AlecPhantom

Dani Healy

Dani Healy Fiction

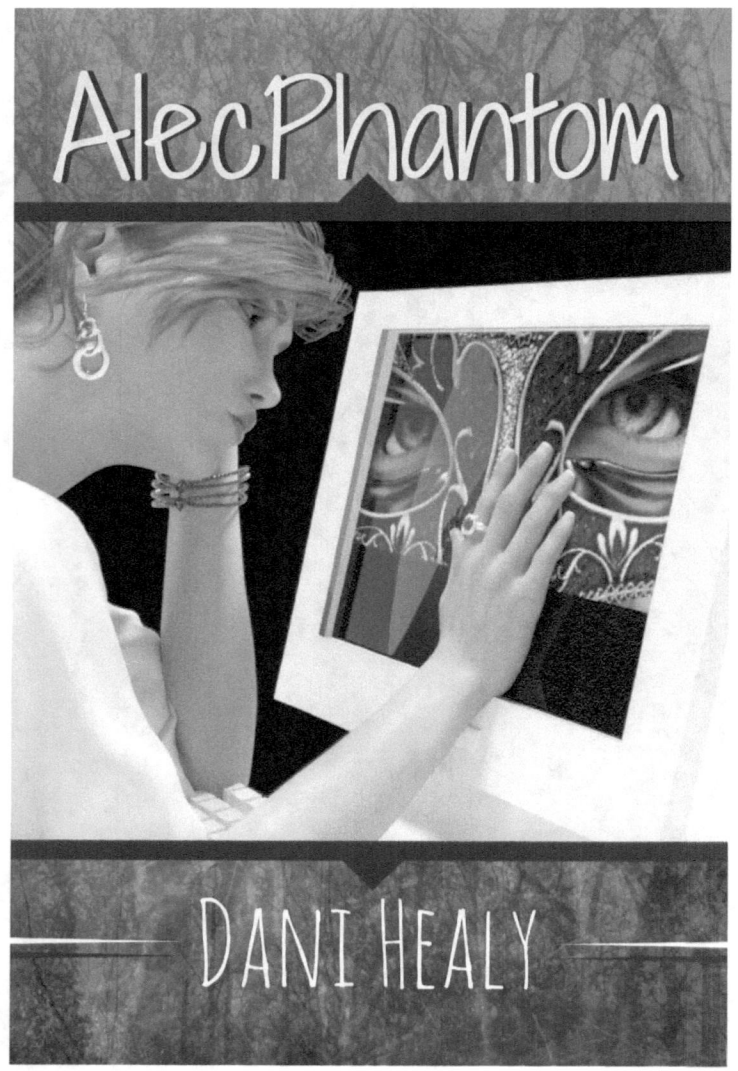

Printed in the United States of America

Character art by Jennie Lyne Hiott

ISBN-10: 0-9987614-0-0

ISBN-13: 978-0-9987614-0-4

Dani Healy Fiction

Dani Healy

<u>DEDICATION</u>

For my wonderful mama…
Not only are you the most amazing mom on the planet, but
you are also my best friend!
You are the woman I will always strive to be.
Thank you for all that you do (the list is far too long).
I love you more than you will ever know!
muah

<u>CHAPTER 1</u>

Let me take you back…

The year was 1998. MTV still played music. VH1 was still cool. Texting did not exist. AOL was the biggest thing to ever hit the planet…at least in my own little bubble. And chat rooms were the best way to meet new people from all over the world.

My name is Scarlett Mitchel, and this is my story…

March 17th, 1998 was the day that I met the elusive, yet intriguing, Alec Cavanaugh.

Five months later…

August 17th 9:52pm CrimsonScar: *Hey there, babe. You around?*
August 17th 9:52pm AlecPhantom: *I am. How was your day, beautiful?*
August 17th 9:53pm CrimsonScar: *It was okay. We were swamped. Apparently, everyone in town ran out of pet supplies on the same day lol I've never seen Let's Get Pets*

that busy for as long as I've been working there...how was your day?

August 17th 9:55pm AlecPhantom: *haha aww, I'm sorry to hear that. As for me...my day was alright. I didn't do much.*

August 17th 9:55pm CrimsonScar: *No work today?*

August 17th 10:02pm AlecPhantom: *No.*

August 17th 10:03pm CrimsonScar: *Ah...are you off again tomorrow?*

August 17th 10:04pm AlecPhantom: *I'm off indefinitely.*

August 17th 10:04pm CrimsonScar: *Why? What happened?*

August 17th 10:10pm AlecPhantom: *Long story.*

August 17th 10:11pm CrimsonScar: *I've got time...*

August 17th 10:15pm AlecPhantom: *Don't really wanna talk about it right now.*

August 17th 10:16pm CrimsonScar: *Um, okay.*

August 17th 10:18pm AlecPhantom: *I'm really tired, so I'm gonna head to bed.*

August 17th 10:19pm CrimsonScar: *Seriously, Alec? We just started chatting!*

August 17th 10:22pm AlecPhantom: *What? I've been waiting around online for the last couple hours.*

August 17th 10:23pm CrimsonScar: *Well, it's not like I meant to be home so late! Can't we talk for a few more minutes?*

August 17th 10:26pm AlecPhantom: *I said I'm tired. Goodnight, Scarlett.*

August 17th 10:27pm CrimsonScar: *Wow, okay then Mr. Grumpus. Whatever. Goodnight.*

AlecPhantom logged out.

I sighed as I slumped against my computer chair. The base squeaked in protest as I leaned back at a slightly awkward angle, clasping my hands above my head. I closed my eyes while grumbling quietly to myself.

"You okay?" a voice called from the hallway.

I glanced up to see my best friend's head peeking around

the corner. "I'm fine," I replied. "Alec is just being an ass tonight. That's all."

"Soooo, nothing new then?" Liza smirked.

My lips turned up on their own accord. "Pretty much."

Liza strolled in and plopped down onto my bed. "What is it with this guy? You've been talking to him via the net for what, like…five months? Why haven't you met in person? Didn't you say he lives like an hour away or something?"

I sighed again as I glanced back at the screen, staring at the short conversation Alec and I had just shared; then I spun around to face her. "I honestly don't know what it is about him. He was so fun and playful…even a bit cocky when we first met, but ever since I suggested that we meet up, it's like…I freaked him out or something." I paused. "I've asked maybe three or four times to meet him in person, but his answer was always no…which made me feel like I was pushing for more than what he was looking for."

Liza covered her legs with my afghan and began tugging on some fraying strands. "What's his reasoning for not wanting to meet then?"

"He says he's not ready for that type of confrontation." I shrugged as if it was no big deal.

It most definitely *was* a big deal.

Liza snorted. "Confrontation? Seriously? Wouldn't it be a meeting or a get-together?"

I pursed my lips and rolled my eyes. "His wording. Not mine."

"What if he's really a chick?" Liza blurted out. She paused and then made a grossed-out face. "Or maybe he's some old dude…who lives in his grandmother's basement…who collects his own belly button lint…and saves it in a jar…"

My face contorted on its own accord. "Oh…gawd…Liza, stop! That's disgusting!"

We both burst into a fit of giggles.

"He's not a chick," I stated once I had composed myself.

"And he has the most amazingly sexy voice. So, there's no way he's a nasty old fart..." I shifted my eyes in her direction. "...who collects his own belly button lint."

Cue another round of giggles.

"Well," Liza stated in an overly serious tone. "Then why does he keep blowing you off?"

I sighed again. "I don't know."

"Oh, God!" Liza suddenly exclaimed. "What if he's married?"

I groaned. "Please don't say things like that!" That particular scenario had not actually entered my mind until that very moment, which was kind of naive on my part.

Liza cocked one of her eyebrows. "Did you ask him?"

I shook my head.

"Well, have you at least seen a picture of him?"

I shook my head again.

In her best Desi Arnaz accent, Liza said, "Well, then Alec has some splainin' to do, Lucy!"

Yes, he does. He really, *really* does.

CHAPTER 2

Tuesday morning, I woke up way before my alarm. Far too many crazy theories were running through my head to allow me to sleep peacefully. Mostly, the terrifying thought that Alec could be married. I shuddered internally.

I made my way into the kitchen where I found Liza leaning against the counter with a coffee cup to her lips.

One look in my direction and she smiled, then handed me her mug. "Looks like you need this more than I do."

I mumbled something that sounded a bit like "thank you" before taking a long slow sip. Then groggily, I shuffled my way back to my room. Of course, I found myself gravitating toward the computer desk, staring at the black screen.

What the hell... I thought to myself. *I might as well get this over with.*

I pressed the power button and downed the rest of my coffee while waiting for the computer to boot up. Then I had the joy of getting dressed while listening to the dialing and screeching sounds as AOL tried to connect. With my toothbrush hanging out of my mouth, I opened up my email and quickly typed a message to Alec, though it would not be filled with our usual back-and-forth playful banter.

I wrote down some of the much-needed questions that Liza had put in my head, and pressed SEND.

From: CrimsonScar
To: AlecPhantom
Date: Tues, Aug 18th, 1998 at 5:37am
Subject: I need to know...

This is probably going to be a little out of nowhere, but I need to know the answers to the following questions, please:

Are you married?

Why won't you send me any pictures of yourself?

Why don't you want to meet me?

Do you live in your grandmother's basement?

There. Done.

I will admit that I chuckled to myself when I wrote the last one.

~*~*~*~

Working in retail while distracted completely sucks!

All day long I had Alec on my mind. I kept imagining that I would go home after work and open his reply. The message would consist of him finally admitting that everything he had told me was a lie; that yes, in fact, he is married...and has like ten kids...and lives in a basement, collecting... *Ugh!*

The only time I was able to think about something else...anything else...was when a customer would rudely interrupt my inner dialogue and force me to help them locate something.

How hard is it to find dog food when the aisle is clearly labeled DOG FOOD? I mean, seriously...come on people!

Not even my co-workers could shake me out of my funk...and believe me, they tried.

Jules and Dave invited me out to lunch; unsurprisingly though, I wasn't very hungry. When we got back, Rue, the sweet older woman who reminded me of my late grandma, covered for me while I had a breakdown in the bathroom. And near the end of my shift, Monica and her sister Charleigh invited Liza and me out for a girls' night. Though, I told them I would have to take a raincheck.

When I arrived home that evening, the first thing I did was make a bee-line straight for my computer. In my rush to get to work on time that morning, I had left the damn thing on. So, when I sat down, I could already see that I had a reply from Alec. It was time-stamped exactly ten minutes after I had sent mine.

Incoming mini panic attack.

I couldn't open it right away. Instead, I sat there staring at the screen as my palms started sweating, and my foot began an anxious tap-dance routine.

A few minutes later, once my body had stopped trembling, I finally managed to hover the cursor directly over his name. His replies were short and to the point, which I already knew they would be. Except for the last one, which he made sure to give slightly more detail.

From: AlecPhantom
To: CrimsonScar
Date: Tues, Aug 18th, 1998 at 5:47am
Subject: Re: I need to know…
　　yaaaaawn Well, good morning to you, too.

Now, to answer the first of your randomly asinine questions… No, I'm not married. Nor have I ever been. Seriously, Scarlett?

As for the pictures. It's pretty simple. You wouldn't like what you see.

The reason we haven't met…see the statement above.

And no, I do not live in my grandmother's basement, or anyone else's basement for that matter. I already told you that I have my own apartment and I live alone. Unless my dog, Sarge, counts as a roommate.

　　grumble grumble

The military-level knot that had been forming in my gut throughout my worry-filled day finally started to unwind. I stared at the screen for a few seconds longer than I needed to, reading and re-reading his reply over and over again to let the words sink in.

He's not married! Thank God! But...I wouldn't like what I see? Why would he say that?

A second or so later, I started the daunting task of going back through my old emails, trying to find the one where he had described what he looked like.

Scrolling...scrolling...scrolling...scroll—AH-HA! March 18th, 1998. The day after we first met.

From: CrimsonScar
To: AlecPhantom
Date: Wed, March 18th, 1998 at 10:05am
Subject: Hi there
I just wanted to say that it was nice chatting with you last night. So, what do you look like? Hair color, eye color, height? We were having such a nice time talking about so many different subjects that I forgot to ask ☺

From: AlecPhantom
To: CrimsonScar
Date: Wed, March 18th, 1998 at 12:10pm
Subject: Re: Hi there
Hey again ☺ I guess I'm pretty average. 6'4", blue eyes, black hair. What do you look like?

From: CrimsonScar
To: AlecPhantom
Date: Wed, March 18th, 1998 at 2:13pm
Subject: Re: Re: Hi there
I'm much shorter than you. I'm 5'5", brown eyes, brown hair. That makes me sound pretty boring lol.

From: AlecPhantom
To: CrimsonScar
Date: Wed, March 18th, 1998 at 3:18pm
Subject: Re: Re: Re: Hi there
Haha, you don't sound boring at all. Quite the opposite actually.

And that was what started it all.
Six-foot-four. Blue eyes. Black hair.
Yep. I was hook-line-and-sunk right from the start.

CHAPTER 3

August 18th 5:57pm AlecPhantom: *Good evening, beautiful.*

August 18th 5:58pm CrimsonScar: *Hello, Alec.*

August 18th 6:05pm AlecPhantom: *Did you get my reply to your email?*

August 18th 6:05pm CrimsonScar: *Yep.*

August 18th 6:07pm AlecPhantom: *And?*

August 18th 6:08pm CrimsonScar: *And... I think I have more questions now than I did before.*

August 18th 6:10pm AlecPhantom: *Of course you do.*

August 18th 6:11pm CrimsonScar: *What the hell is wrong with you?*

August 18th 6:13pm AlecPhantom: *Look, I'm sorry I was a jerk last night okay?! So, can you stop with the third degree?*

August 18th 6:14pm CrimsonScar: *Sounds like you're still being a jerk!*

August 18th 6:17pm AlecPhantom: *Are you busy at the moment?*

August 18th 6:18pm CrimsonScar: *No...why?*

AlecPhantom logged out.

"You have *got* to be kidding me!" I said out loud.

Just as I was about to throw a not-so-ladylike tantrum, my house phone started to ring…which also disconnected my internet connection. Yay for dial-up!

One glance at the caller ID and I instantly smiled. "Hey."

Alec sighed on his end of the line. "Hi, Scarlett."

I could just imagine him sitting there with his head in his hands, his eyes closed, frustration covering his face. If only I knew what the features of his face actually looked like.

"Hi, Alec."

"I'm sorry," he told me. And I could tell by the tone of his voice that he meant it.

I plopped down on my bed, twirling the phone cord around my fingers. "I know," I sighed. "Me, too."

"You have nothing to be sorry for. I know I'm not the easiest person to put up with, but I'm thankful that you do."

I smiled at his words. Mostly because they were entirely true. He really wasn't the easiest person to deal with…but what could I say? I loved the guy. *Whoa. Did I just admit to myself…? Yeah. I totally did.*

I cleared my throat. "So, um…about my questions…?"

"Yeah?"

"Why did you say I wouldn't like what I'd see? Did you lie about your appearance or something?"

"No," he replied softly.

A few agonizingly long seconds passed without another word.

I sighed again. "If you lied, it's okay…I just want…"

"I didn't," he interjected. "I haven't lied about anything."

"So, you're really six-foot-four?"

He sighed once more. "Yeah."

Good. 'Cuz I totally dig tall guys. "And you have blue eyes?"

"Yes, Scarlett. I do."

11

"And bl...?"

"And black hair," he finished for me. "Yes."

I blew out my breath slowly as I sat up on my bed. "Then why would you say that?"

He mimicked my sigh and remained quiet, other than exhaling deeply a few more times.

"Alec..."

"You just wouldn't, okay?!" His tone was suddenly clipped with annoyance.

I could feel my irritation rising as well. "That's not an answer!"

"Well, it's the only one I have for you!"

Our conversation was clearly going nowhere. Again. And with every passing second, I was becoming more and more frustrated with him. *Why is this man so hell-bent on avoiding such a simple question?*

A second or so later, I ended up doing something childish.

I hung up on him.

And much to my surprise, he did not call back.

CHAPTER 4

Wednesday morning, there was still no word from Alec, but I was honestly too pissed-off at him to truly care. Though, when I got home from work, the first thing I did was turn on my computer to check AOL's instant messenger, AIM for short.

I paced anxiously around my room, constantly checking the screen as the usual connecting sounds filtered through the speakers.

I will admit that it was somewhat of a surprise not to see him logged on and waiting for me like he always had been for the past five months. The sick feeling that had been swirling around in my stomach for the past couple days was making me extra anxious.

I quickly checked my email, because surely he had sent me something there.

Nope.

Zip. Zilch. Nadda.

Lastly, I checked the answering machine. I could see the red light blinking from across the room, showing that I had one unheard message. I smiled as I pressed PLAY, but my hopes were immediately crushed when I realized that it was just a telemarketer.

That night, I ate dinner with Liza in silence. We had been best friends since we were kids, and roommates for the last three years, so she knew me well enough not to pry. Not when I was about two milliseconds away from having a complete meltdown.

~*~*~*~

While I was standing at the sink washing dishes, because it was my night, Liza came up beside me and bumped my hip.

I shook my soapy hands at her face in response, flinging bubbles all over the place.

She giggled and swatted at me playfully before joining in to help me dry some plates. "You alright?"

I sighed and took a pause. "Yeah, I guess so."

Liza mimicked my sigh. "Boys are stupid," she grumbled.

I snort-laughed and bumped her hip back. "Yep. Pretty much."

<u>CHAPTER 5</u>

Thursday morning, I didn't even bother turning on my computer. I honestly didn't see a need when I already knew that Alec wasn't going to write me.

Maybe I shouldn't have pushed him like I did. I let out a deep sigh as I gathered up my purse and car keys before heading out the door.

Throughout my day at work, idiots were everywhere.

This person couldn't find this.

That person spilled that.

Someone else didn't understand that the customer is *not* always right, no matter what the stupid saying is!

Simple tasks morphed into complicated messes at every turn. Not even sharing my shift with Dave and Jules could save my sanity, and those two were like the store's class-clowns.

So, when the time came for me to clock out, I literally bolted out the front door.

~*~*~*~

While running errands after my hectic day, I tried to convince myself that I knew Alec better than anyone and that he would eventually come around…however, the sad truth was, I didn't know much about him at all.

The only supposed facts I had were, that he was twenty-seven years old, which was only three years older than me. He was born and raised in Deerfield Beach, Florida. His parents' names are Lindy and Henry, and he has an older sister named Cora.

But who is he really? Who is the man hiding behind his computer, talking to me on a daily basis, yet refusing to connect beyond a fifteen-inch screen? What makes him tick? And why is he constantly on the verge of exploding when I press for what should be straightforward answers to common questions?

On the short drive back home, I put on some music as loud as my crappy car speakers would allow. I guess I was hoping that the booming bass would drown out the voice in the back of my head that kept saying, *he is definitely hiding something from you.*

That evening, after having a quick bite to eat with Liza and her boyfriend, Derek, at our local Pizza Hut, I rushed through a shower and forced myself to walk past the invisible neon sign that was flashing above my computer.

OVER HERE SCARLETT! CHECK ME! MESSAGE HIM!

~*~*~*~

I tossed and turned for nearly three hours before heaving my groggy body out of bed. I reluctantly sauntered into the living room and found myself sitting on the couch in complete darkness. A few minutes went by as I stared out the window of our quaint little condo, watching the cars passing by on the semi-busy street.

The gentle hum of the refrigerator gave me another chance at distraction. I strolled into the kitchen and opened every single cabinet…twice…before finally making a decision. *Cheese and Ritz it is!*

I made a plateful of cracker sandwiches and then headed back to my room. I turned on the little light next to my bed and grabbed a novel at random off the bookshelf beside my desk...'Cujo' by Stephen King. Always a classic.

I got cozy beneath my covers, using my chest as a table, and began to munch and read.

It really is amazing how the human mind works. When we are entirely preoccupied with something, our brain just can't seem to focus on anything else. I realized this incredible fact when I read the same sentence at least thirty times, and yet still couldn't remember what it said.

As the last bite of cheese and cracker made it past my lips, my eyes shifted towards my computer. *Ah...what the hell; I might as well get the disappointment over with.*

I climbed out of bed and headed over to my desk, placing my plate and my book right next to the monitor. I booted up the computer and impatiently waited for it to fully load.

The typical screeching sound as AOL tried to connect was as loud as a foghorn, so I quickly turned down the volume in the hope that I hadn't woken Liza up.

No sign of Alec on AIM. Though, I was not surprised. It was nearly three in the morning after all. I typed in my email and password, then swallowed nervously as I hit ENTER. The sick feeling in my stomach instantly disappeared when I heard the familiar sound of, "You've Got Mail!" I deleted a few spam messages, and then noticed that I had a new email from Alec.

Thank God!

From: AlecPhantom
To: CrimsonScar
Date: Thurs, Aug 20th, 1998 at 3:18pm
Subject: I'm an idiot
I think the subject line pretty much says it all. We should talk. I promise not to be an asshole.
P.S. I miss your voice.

I closed my eyes and let out a sigh of relief. *I miss your voice, too, Alec.*

The next thing I knew, I had the receiver in my hand, and the line was ringing. When his sleepy voice answered, I instantly melted into a puddle.

"Sorry I woke you," I whispered.

"Scarlett?" He suddenly sounded fully awake and alert.

"The one and only..."

He sighed, and I heard shuffling sounds on his end of the line. I could only assume that he was untangling himself from his cocoon of blankets. "I'm glad you called," he whispered. "I've been thinking about you a lot since..."

He didn't have to finish. I knew exactly what was running through his mind. "I know." I sighed. "Same here. I shouldn't have hung up on you, I just..."

"No," he interrupted me. "I was a jerk." He sighed again. "You had every right to..."

Cue the awkward silence.

A short while later, I blurted out, "So, what are you doing for Halloween?" In my mind, I instantly face-palmed myself. In an attempt to recover, I added, "I know it's not for a couple of months, but I thought that maybe we could..." A nervous laugh stopped my words.

Alec let out a soft chuckle. "I haven't made any plans yet." He paused. "Why?" The tone of his voice sounded like a mixture of curiosity and reluctance.

"Well...every year, management throws a Halloween Ball. And yes, I said a ball." I paused in case he wanted to make some smart-assed comment. He didn't. So, I continued, "It may sound silly, but it's actually a lot of fun...and it raises some money for the local pet shelters, so even if it is a bit outdated to attend a Halloween party, Liza and I always go. The CEO of Let's Get Pets rents out a building that looks like a castle from a fantasy world. Like one of those amazing pictures straight out of a magazine from Ireland or something. There are these thick velvet curtains that cover the floor to ceiling windows, and the black marble floors are just so beautiful. I always feel like

I've been transported back in time when I'm there…" I began pacing as I nervously rambled on and on about all the previous parties, giving way too many unnecessary details, but I just could not seem to control my mouth. In my mind, I had said, *hush, Scarlett…stop talking for two seconds*, but alas, I continued on.

Alec remained quiet; allowing me to talk his ear off for God-only-knows how long.

When I finally took a breath, I forced myself to be quiet and wait for a reply.

Alec cleared his throat. "Well, that sounds absolutely lovely, Scarlett…but I don't know if it's a good idea."

I sighed heavily. "Why not?"

"I already told you," he replied matter-of-factly.

"Seriously, Alec? What the hell are you hiding?"

"I'm not hiding anything!" he retorted.

My voice raised. "That's bullshit! Either you're keeping something from me, or you just don't want to meet me. And if this is all we will ever be…two voices on the phone or two names on a screen, then…I don't think I can do this anymore!"

"You…you can't do what anymore?" he asked worriedly.

Even I could not believe the next words that came out of my mouth. I sighed painfully. "If you're not willing to ever see me face to face, then I don't think we should continue to talk anymore."

"Scarlett, don't say that!" he blurted out.

I blew out my breath as I fell backward onto my bed. "It's just…it seems pointless if our relationship is leading nowhere, doesn't it? I want more than just an online conversation with you, Alec…and you know that."

"We can figure something out," he said quickly. "I don't want to lose you."

I closed my eyes and tightened my grip on the phone. "Then say yes. Tell me you'll meet me at this stupid Halloween Ball. Tell me that we can finally be more than just our screen names."

The silence that followed was so loud…and dragged on for so long…that I could hardly stand it. But I didn't dare break it first.

Finally, his whispered response made it to my ears. "Okay…"

I instantly sat up. Though, it took a second or two for me to comprehend that he had just agreed to meet me. "Really? You're not going to back out or change your mind last minute?"

"I am a man of my word," he replied confidently. "But, Scarlett… I just… Don't expect… It's not like I'm…"

He never did manage to get a full sentence out.

I could not stand the fact that he seemed so uncomfortable about the whole thing. "Alec, if you are who you claim to be, and you haven't lied about anything, then you have nothing to worry about."

He sighed yet again. "You just don't understand. It's complicated."

"It's only complicated because you're making it that way!" I stated sternly.

CHAPTER 6

Two months later...

Alec had not been around much the last couple of months. I told myself it was because he was busy looking for a new job, but in the back of my mind, I knew the truth. He was avoiding me because of my ultimatum.

Shortly after he agreed to meet, I sent him a picture of my dress while it was hanging on the back of my closet door. The bodice was a red and black lace corset with long velvet sleeves that would barely cover my shoulders. The slit on the side of the skirt nearly came up to my hip. I had hoped that seeing it would not only give him some idea of what he should choose to wear, but also to excite him about the prospect of seeing me wearing it. But his only reply was, "It looks nice."

It. Looks. Nice.

I received a few instant messages after that which consisted of the phrases, "*Hey, how are you? Just checking in*", and the occasional, "*Thinking of you*", but that was it. I was beginning to question my own judgment by that point.

Though, with my life not entirely consumed by Alec anymore, Liza and I had gotten to spend some extra time together again. Mondays through Thursdays, our nights went back to vegging out on the couch while watching reruns of 'I Love Lucy', 'Bewitched', and 'I Dream of Jeannie' while reenacting random scenes with fake British accents. I don't know why we found that so amusing, but we always ended up laughing so hard that we couldn't see…or breathe. Who needs air, right?

Fridays, we collected on Monica and Charleigh's raincheck invitation.

Saturdays were Liza's usual date night with her boyfriend, Derek, so those evenings I just curled up with a good book and lost myself in my favorite love stories.

Sundays were back to our old board game nights. Don't Wake Daddy was probably one of the silliest games for two women in their twenties to be playing…but that didn't even compare to Hungry Hungry Hippos.

Liza had a tendency to let her inner child take over. During each game, she would get overly enthusiastic and start to hit the lever on the hippo's butt so hard that all the little marbles would fly off the tray, then sail through the air like mini projectiles, and end up rolling around all over the floor. In her mind, that meant she had won. I guess our version should be renamed Hungry Marble Flinging Lady.

In the middle of one of our marble-pick-up sessions, Liza asked the same question she had been asking for the past few weeks. "So, what are you gonna do if Alec doesn't show up?"

I sighed as I crawled underneath the coffee table to retrieve a tiny white ball. "He'll show," I grumbled.

"But what if he doesn't?" Liza's face suddenly appeared on the other side of the table as she laid down to grab the marble that I was reaching for.

"Hey!" I exclaimed. I wiggled backwards to get up off the floor and miscalculated the clearance. I bonked my head right on the side of the solid oak table. "Ouch! Dammit!" I rubbed my throbbing head and sighed again. "Look, I know you are just trying to prepare me for the worst possible outcome, but please, Liza…" I paused and sighed once more, mostly from the ache spreading throughout my skull. "Please stop asking me that. You're making me extra anxious…and you probably just gave me a concussion."

Liza sighed and gently tapped the top of my head. "I'm sorry…on both accounts."

~*~*~*~

Just ten days before the Halloween Ball, a man in an expensively tailored suit showed up at our door holding a package under his arm.

When I appeared in the doorway, he cleared his throat and smiled sweetly. "Excuse my intrusion, but I have a delivery for a…" he paused to glance down, "…Miss Scarlett Mitchel."

"Oh, um…that would be me," I replied.

The man smiled wider as he handed me the package and turned to leave without saying another word.

I glanced down. There was an envelope taped to the box with my name written neatly on the front…no sender's name listed, only a return address. "Who sent this?" I asked curiously.

The man glanced back over his shoulder and tipped his hat. "I'm afraid I'm not at liberty to say. Have a lovely day, miss." Then he got into his vehicle and drove away.

"Who was that?" Liza asked after I closed the front door.

I shrugged. "No idea."

She puckered her lips. "Secret admirer?"

I stuck my tongue out in her direction and made a few incoherent noises while opening the envelope.

Inside was a note in the same unfamiliar handwriting.

My dearest Scarlett,

I had this custom made after seeing your dress. Mine completes the set, so we will be able to find each other in the crowd. By the time you receive this, I will have sent a picture to your email. See you soon.

P.S. I begged Liza for your home address. Please don't be mad at her.

Yours always, Alec

I glanced up at my best friend. "You knew who sent this!" I scolded playfully.

Liza grinned. "What can I say? When he told me his plan, I couldn't say no. Apparently I'm a closet romantic. Who knew?"

I smiled as I curiously dug through the pink packing peanuts until my fingers landed on something rough, feeling a bit like sandpaper. A gasp escaped my lips as I stared down at a beautiful red and black filigree mask. Fake diamonds lined above the eyes and black lace ran along the entire bottom of the mask.

I immediately headed to my room to check my email. Sure enough, there was a message from Alec…with an attachment. *How did he know I had received the package already?*

Nervous butterflies filled my stomach as I clicked DOWNLOAD.

Slowly but surely, an image started to load.

The top of a man's head appeared…jet black hair.

The butterflies started to grow stronger as more of the image came into view.

A mask with the same filigree pattern as mine, except in black and silver, started to load, but this one was much larger. Mine only covered my eyes and nose; this one covered his whole face. Very masculine and mysterious, and completely unfair.

My breath suddenly caught in my throat as Alec's beautiful eyes stared back at me through the small cutouts.

Eyes so blue that they seemed unreal.

My hand reflexively reached for the screen, caressing his masked face as if he could feel my touch.

The old saying *"The Eyes Are The Window To The Soul"* popped into my head. If those words held any truth, then Alec must have the most captivating and beautiful soul imaginable.

I quickly grabbed the phone and dialed his number, which simultaneously disconnected my internet.

He answered on the third ring. "Hey, Scar…"

"I got your package today," I blurted out.

"I know." He paused and chuckled softly.

"How…?"

"The man who delivered it works for my father, so after he left your house, he called me."

I smiled to myself. "Very clever, Mr. Phantom."

Alec laughed. "Dare I ask what you thought?"

"The mask is lovely. I didn't expect you to do that."

"That's why it's called a surprise."

"And I saw your picture." My words came out as a whisper, though I had not meant for them to.

He audibly gulped on his end of the line.

"Your eyes, Alec…" I took a deep breath and let it out slowly. "They literally took my breath away."

His intake of air was swift, then he sighed. "Now you know for sure that I haven't lied," he whispered.

I was still staring at his photo while speaking to him. I just could not look away. "Will you send me one without the mask?"

His reply was immediate. "No."

CHAPTER 7

Five days before the ball, Alec and I resumed talking on AIM. Which was a nice change of pace after all the silence he had been giving me.

The best part was, things between us had gone back to the way it was in the beginning. Playful and sweet.

October 26th 12:05pm CrimsonScar: *Hey, you here?*
October 26th 12:07pm AlecPhantom: *Nope...*
October 26th 12:08pm CrimsonScar: *lol smart ass!*
October 26th 12:08pm AlecPhantom: *lol that's me! What are you doing home so early on a Monday?*
October 26th 12:09pm CrimsonScar: *Ugh! How much time ya got?*
October 26th 12:10pm AlecPhantom: *I'm all ears.*
October 26th 12:11pm CrimsonScar: *Well, that's an image I'll never be able to get out of my head.*
October 26th 12:13pm AlecPhantom: *haha! Now who's the smart ass?*
October 26th 12:14pm CrimsonScar: *lol...well, I need some*

laughs after my day! And you are my only outlet right now since Liza is still at work!

October 26ᵗʰ 12:17pm AlecPhantom: *Using me for my sense of humor? I guess I'm okay with that lol so, what happened?*

October 26ᵗʰ 12:24pm CrimsonScar: **sigh* Well, it started off pretty good, but about an hour into my shift, Jules noticed that two of the fish tanks were leaking in the aquatic section, so a few of us ran over to move the fish into new tanks and to drain the ones that were dripping. Everything seemed to be going just fine after that until one of the newbies got the brilliant idea to climb to the top of one of the back shelves to retrieve something for a customer. His added weight ended up being too much, knocking over the entire shelving unit...and guess what it slammed into? The brand-new, floor to ceiling, freshwater tank...full of the most expensive fish in the store!*

October 26ᵗʰ 12:26pm AlecPhantom: *Omg!*

October 26ᵗʰ 12:27pm CrimsonScar: *Yeeeeeeah! Water and fish were literally EVERYWHERE! It was a mad dash to find and save all the slippery, flipping, flopping creatures. Then amidst the rescue chaos, I got bit by one of the baby sharks while I was trying to transport it into a new tank! Yep, that's my luck. Bit by a shark...on dry land...in a friggin' pet store!*

October 26ᵗʰ 12:28pm AlecPhantom: **mouth drops open* lol Wow! Are you okay?*

October 26ᵗʰ 12:29pm CrimsonScar: *Yeah, I'm alright lol. My boss sent me to the hospital to have the wound disinfected, and I ended up getting two little stitches...plus a tetanus shot. And you know my fear of needles! *shudders**

October 26ᵗʰ 12:30pm AlecPhantom: *Oh, Scarlett, I am so sorry! I wish I could have been there to hold your hand.*

October 26ᵗʰ 12:31pm CrimsonScar: *Aww I wish that, too, but that would require us to have met already...soooo lol.*

October 26ᵗʰ 12:35pm AlecPhantom: *You just won't let that* *go, will you? lol.*

October 26th 12:37pm CrimsonScar: *Not a chance lol.*

October 26th 12:40pm AlecPhantom: *Hey, I said yes...eventually! lol And in 5 days it will happen...*

October 26th 12:41pm CrimsonScar: *I know! And I'm so damn excited!*

October 26th 12:43pm AlecPhantom: *I know you are.*

October 26th 12:46pm CrimsonScar: **loving glare* Aren't you?*

October 26th 12:47pm AlecPhantom: *haha glaring at me now, eh?*

October 26th 12:48pm CrimsonScar: *Don't tempt me into standing you up at the ball, Mr. Phantom!*

October 26th 12:50pm AlecPhantom: *lol would you think me less of a man if I admit that my heart dropped when you said that?*

October 26th 12:51pm CrimsonScar: *I would never think less of you.*

October 26th 12:52pm AlecPhantom: *You know I'm excited to see you, Scarlett. It's just very...complicated on my end.*

October 26th 12:52pm CrimsonScar: **sigh* yeah, you've said that...but I still don't understand why.*

October 26th 12:54pm AlecPhantom: *I know you don't.*

October 26th 12:54pm CrimsonScar: *You're seriously not gonna tell me why you're so uncomfortable about this?*

October 26th 12:56pm AlecPhantom: *Nope. You'll find out soon enough.*

October 26th 12:57pm CrimsonScar: *Ya know, when we are finally face to face, I'm gonna hug you so tight that you won't be able to breathe! Then you won't be worrying about whatever is making you feel so uneasy!*

October 26th 1:01pm AlecPhantom: *LOL I won't be able to breathe? Aren't you supposed to be making me want to meet you? Attempted murder kinda puts a damper on the* *fun aspect of all this.*

October 26th 1:03pm CrimsonScar: *hahaha Okay then...what if I promise not to impede your breathing? Does that make our meeting any more appealing?*

October 26th 1:04pm AlecPhantom: *lol Much more, thanks...I think.*

October 26th 1:05pm CrimsonScar: *You're welcome...I think lol.*

October 26th 1:17pm AlecPhantom: *lol well, I hate to cut this chat short, but I just got some unexpected company. Can we talk later?*

October 26th 1:19pm CrimsonScar: *Uh, yeah sure. I should get some housework done anyway. Have fun, babe!*

October 26th 1:20pm AlecPhantom: *Thanks. Speak to you soon, beautiful.*

AlecPhantom logged out.

~*~*~*~

October 26th 7:32pm AlecPhantom: *Boo!*

October 26th 7:47pm CrimsonScar: *Ahhh! lol Sorry for the delay...was eating dinner with Liza.*

October 26th 7:48pm AlecPhantom: *No worries. Your tummy full and happy?*

October 26th 7:50pm CrimsonScar: *haha yep! Is your company gone?*

October 26th 7:50pm AlecPhantom: *Yeah. I honestly didn't think they would stay that long.*

October 26th 7:51pm CrimsonScar: *Aww lol, well as long as you guys had fun, that's what matters!*

October 26th 7:53pm AlecPhantom: *lol yeah, we did. They all wanted to go out tonight, but I told them I already had plans.*

October 26th 7:54pm CrimsonScar: *Oh? What sort of plans might those be?*

October 26th 7:55pm AlecPhantom: **nonchalant wave* Oh, ya know...just hanging out with my favorite person.*

October 26th 7:55pm CrimsonScar: *Sarge?*

October 26th 7:57pm AlecPhantom: **snort laughter* A non-furry person!*

October 26th 7:57pm CrimsonScar: *LOL good answer.*

October 26th 7:58pm AlecPhantom: *Why thank you! *bows* I have my moments lol.*

October 26th 7:59pm CrimsonScar: *Yes, you do...ish.*

October 26th 8:01pm AlecPhantom: *Ohh! You're gonna 'ish' me now?*

October 26th 8:02pm CrimsonScar: *Yup! What cha gonna do about it?*

October 26th 8:02pm AlecPhantom: *You'll find out when we meet.*

October 26th 8:03pm CrimsonScar: *I'm not sure if I should be excited or terrified right now.*

October 26th 8:05pm AlecPhantom: *haha now you know how I felt when you threatened to strangle-hug me in our last conversation!*

October 26th 8:06pm CrimsonScar: *lol a strangle-hug? Wow, Alec...you definitely have a way with words!*

October 26th 8:06pm AlecPhantom: *Hmm, ish?*

October 26th 8:07pm CrimsonScar: *No 'ish' this time lol.*

October 26th 8:08pm AlecPhantom: *Ha! Then I'm gonna take that as a compliment!*

October 26th 8:09pm CrimsonScar: *You go right on ahead lol. Well, I guess it's my turn to cut the conversation short. Liza is calling me for an unplanned game night.*

October 26th 8:11pm AlecPhantom: *HA! Hungry Hungry Hippos?*

October 26th 8:11pm CrimsonScar: *LOL I sure hope not. My head still hurts from the last time. I think I'll request fifty-two pick up instead.*

October 26th 8:15pm AlecPhantom: *So, your choices are...a brain injury or multiple papercuts?*

October 26th 8:15pm CrimsonScar: *hahaha pretty much!*

October 26th 8:16pm AlecPhantom: *I'll bring some ice and Band-Aids to the ball...ya know, just in case.*

October 26th 8:17pm CrimsonScar: *Aww, aren't you sweet...*

October 26th 8:18pm AlecPhantom: *The dots suggest that you don't really mean it!*

October 26th 8:19pm CrimsonScar: *Hmm...I think I'll just leave you wondering.*

October 26th 8:22pm AlecPhantom: *Not nice, Scarlett...not nice at all!*

October 26th 8:23pm CrimsonScar: *haha gotta love me!*

October 26th 8:23pm AlecPhantom: **grumble grumble**

October 26th 8:24pm CrimsonScar: *Crazy man lol.*

October 26th 8:25pm AlecPhantom: **mimics you* gotta love me!*

October 26th 8:25pm CrimsonScar: *Ish...*

October 26th 8:26pm AlecPhantom: **sigh* that is just plain wrong!*

October 26th 8:27pm CrimsonScar: *LOL I'm sowwy!*

October 26th 8:27pm AlecPhantom: *Uh huh lol.*

October 26th 8:28pm CrimsonScar: *So, you don't regret staying home tonight do you?*

October 26th 8:30pm AlecPhantom: *Um? That wasn't random or anything lol.*

October 26th 8:31pm CrimsonScar: *lol...well, I mean, you didn't go out so we could talk...and now I'm leaving after a very short chat.*

October 26th 8:32pm AlecPhantom: *Scarlett, you know that I enjoy all of our conversations, no matter the length.*

October 26th 8:33pm CrimsonScar: *Are you sure? Maybe you could still meet up with your friends?*

October 26th 8:34pm AlecPhantom: *Naa, they'll be fine*

without me...and I'm kinda tired anyway, so I'll probably just download a couple songs from Napster and call it an early night. Don't worry your pretty little head. Go enjoy your time with Liza.

October 26th 8:35pm CrimsonScar: *Thanks, Alec.*

October 26th 8:35pm AlecPhantom: *No thanks needed. Goodnight, beautiful.*

October 26th 8:36pm CrimsonScar: *Goodnight. Sweet dreams.*

October 26th 8:37pm AlecPhantom: *You, too.*

AlecPhantom logged out.

CHAPTER 8

Five days later...

The night I had been waiting for finally arrived.

Liza and I were running around like chickens with their heads cut off, trying to get ready for the Halloween Ball while blasting UB40 through my little boombox speakers.

Two girls, plus one small bathroom, equaled slight scheduling complications. Thankfully, though, it was my turn to hog the mirror.

"Phone is for you!" Liza called out.

I groaned as I put down my eyeliner. "If you're using that as a trick to get me out of the bathroom, I'm not falling for it!"

Liza laughed. "It's Alec."

I made my way to the living room where Liza stood, holding out the phone.

"Take your tiiiiiime," she said sweetly in a sing-songy tone while grinning from ear to ear.

I eyed her suspiciously, half expecting the line to be a dial tone when I put the receiver to my ear…because my best friend was a jokester like that. "Hello?"

"Hi, Scarlett."

I instantly smiled. "Hey, Alec."

"I can't help falling in love with you."

My eyes widened. "What?"

Alec chuckled. "The song you're listening to."

"Oh," I cleared my throat as a nervous laugh escaped. "Yeah. It's one of my favorites."

"Mine, too," he replied. Then after a few seconds of silence, he continued, "I just wanted to let you know that I'm leaving now...ya know, since I live over an hour away. I want to make sure I get there around the time that you will...and give myself some extra time in case I get lost." He laughed softly.

I nearly melted into a puddle from how adorable he sounded. "I can't wait to see you!"

There was a slight pause before he replied, "Me, too."

"Drive safe, okay?"

"Thank you, Scarlett. I will. You do the same."

~*~*~*~

"We. Are. So. Late!" I grumbled irritatingly. My purse was clutched tightly in my lap as my feet began to fidget impatiently in the passenger seat of Liza's car.

"I'm sorry," Liza whined. "Blame my shoes for not matching my dress like they were supposed to!"

I rolled my eyes so hard that I could have sworn I saw my brain. "Your dress is black...the shoes were black!"

"The shoes were charcoal!" Liza argued. "They would have clashed!"

I let out a growl-like sigh and turned toward the window, watching as the final piece of the setting sun disappeared into the horizon. "If Alec decided to leave because of your stupid non-black-charcoal shoes, I'm literally gonna kill you...and since it's Halloween, everyone will believe it's fake blood!"

Liza chuckled and gunned the engine a little more.

"Okay, Scarlett, you're starting to scare me a little bit."

I grumbled under my breath as she repeatedly apologized again and again.

A few minutes later, I cried out, "SLOW DOWN! Turn here! Turn here!"

"Oh, my gosh! I know!" Liza quipped. "I've been here before too, remember?" The vehicle started to coast to the left. "Geez, Scar, you gotta calm down! You nearly gave me a heart attack screaming like that!"

My frustration toward my best friend was instantly replaced with a nervousness that nearly had me trembling from head to toe.

Liza veered into the parking lot and pulled into what appeared to be the last remaining parking space. After shifting the car into park, she turned toward me. "Can you help me zip up my...? Hey, Scarlett! Wait for me, dammit!"

My best friend's voice faded away as I raced across the asphalt toward the castle-like building. The sound of my heels clicking on the ground sounded like a mini machine gun...tap tap tap tap tap tap tap.

I only slowed my pace when I reached the walkway. As I approached the front doors, I blew out my breath and shook out my hands to try and relieve some of the jitters that were taking over my body...but nothing seemed to help.

Had time allowed, I would have stood there for a few more minutes until I was able to gather myself, but thanks to Liza and her stupid, I'm-going-to-burn-them-when-I-get-home shoes, I couldn't do that.

So, I adjusted my mask with trembling hands, making sure that it was perfectly in place before I reached for the handle. Inside, the ball was already in full swing. I groaned as I scanned the enormous room. *How the hell am I supposed to find Alec in this chaos?*

Liza finally caught up to me, semi out of breath. "Have you found him yet?"

I sighed and turned to look at her, my face deadpan. "I

literally walked in the door two minutes before you did…so no, I haven't found him."

Liza placed her hands on my shoulders and put her face an inch away from mine. "Just relax and breathe. He's here somewhere."

"Yeah…somewhere," I grumbled. "Or he already left because he thinks I stood him up!" *I never should have joked about that!* I shrugged her off as I stood on my tip-toes, anxiously scanning the faces around me.

More often than not, I was able to overlook my best friend's inability to show up on time, but that particular night was super important; so, I was more than a little peeved that she and her stupid-ass-shoes may have very well ruined it.

Liza rolled her eyes and sighed dramatically. "I can only apologize so many times!"

I ignored her and continued searching the crowd. Some faces I recognized; most of them I didn't, because they were hidden behind different types of Halloween masks.

~*~*~*~

At least three songs had played since our arrival, and there was still no sign of Alec anywhere.

I happened to come across Rue and her husband, who were wearing matching doctor outfits. I said a brief hello and then bumped into Monica, who was decked out from head to toe in white like an angel, while ironically grinding against Jules, who was dressed as a devil. I shook my head and smiled when they waved at me.

I slowly made my way through the maze of bodies with Liza close behind, still profusely apologizing, but I stopped dead in my tracks when I caught a glimpse of a familiar mask on the opposite side of the room. My heart somehow managed to end up in my throat…at least it felt that way with it beating completely out of control.

My face must have gone pale or something, because Liza finally stopped talking and followed my stare. "Oh, my gosh!" she blurted out. "Is that him?"

I managed a small nod in response.

"Well, then here's your moment!" she said cheerfully. "Now go…go!"

I tried to take a step, really I did, but I could not seem to move. My feet felt as though they were literally glued to the floor.

A second or so later, Liza's hands were on my shoulders, gently pushing me forward. "Go!" she said again.

My feet finally obeyed just as the music changed. In the same moment, Alec seemed to notice me. He and I didn't take our eyes off each other as we weaved through the crowded dance floor.

As if destined by fate, 'Can't Fight This Feeling' by REO Speedwagon began to filter through the speakers all around the room. Listening to the words while watching Alec gracefully walking toward me, caused my heart to stutter.

Little did I know, those words would end up having more meaning than I could have ever expected.

My cheeks were starting to hurt from trying to hide my ever-growing smile…and I nearly tripped a few times, causing my exposed face to redden.

Unfortunately, I could not see Alec's reaction behind the full-face mask he was wearing, but I just assumed that he was smiling at me and my awkward clumsiness.

Soon, he and I were only a foot or so apart.

Two more strides of his long legs brought him directly in front of me. And my poor heart continued to hammer in my chest, resounding in my ears.

"You're here," I whispered breathlessly.

He inhaled deeply, then let it out slowly. "I promised I would be," he replied quietly.

Hearing his voice in person nearly sent me over the edge. I could not believe that he was finally within reach.

I was so awestruck that a small burst of air expelled from my mouth. "When I was late…I just assumed…"

He chuckled softly and crossed his arms, molding the

dark material of his jacket to his upper body. "You thought I would run the first chance I got?"

I smiled and bit my lip while briefly looking away. "Something like that."

Alec leaned in closer. His body so close, yet so far away. As I breathed him in, the fragrance of his cologne instantly intoxicated me.

"I told you, Scarlett..." his deep voice crooned. "I am a man of my word." Without any hesitation, his strong hands gently pulled me into his embrace.

The next thing I knew, my entire body began to tremble all over again. I guess the shock of actually being in his arms sent each of my senses into overload. I linked my hands behind his back for some sort of stability and leaned my head against his chest.

As if he could read my mind, Alec wrapped his arms around my waist and tightened his hold on me, exhaling slowing as he leaned his head against mine. "I got you," he whispered.

We stood there holding onto one another. We didn't dance. We didn't move. It was as if we were the only people in the room. As if the world around us no longer existed.

The music in the background slowly began to fade away as Alec gently trailed his fingers up and down the middle of my back.

A split second later, he raised one of his arms in the air as if to signal the DJ. There was a slight pause in the music as a ping of static filtered through the speakers; then 'You're The Inspiration' by Chicago started to play.

I glanced up and gave Alec a questioning stare. "Friend of yours?" I asked curiously.

"Not exactly." He let out a soft laugh. "While I was waiting for you to arrive, the DJ and I talked for a while. I told him a little bit about our situation and how special tonight was. He said to give him a signal, and he would play any song I wanted...just for you. This was the one I chose."

A shy smile made its way across my lips. "It's perfect," I whispered.

Alec started singing along quietly so that only I could hear.

I leaned my head back against his chest and sighed as his angelic voice sent me into a blissfully hypnotic trance.

CHAPTER 9

The melody slowly faded, and couples began dispersing to the dining area. I turned to follow the crowd, but Alec grasped hold of my wrist to stop me.

"Before we sit down to eat, there's something you need to know."

"Oh?" I replied timidly.

Without any other explanation, he took my hand and ushered me into a darkened corner away from everyone else. When we were finally alone, and out of earshot from all the other guests, he said, "Before anything else happens tonight, I need to get something off my chest…or in this case, I need to stop hiding behind my mask."

I could tell by the distressed tone of his voice, that whatever was about to come out of his mouth was going to be intense.

A million things raced through my mind. "Okay…" I said hesitantly. "What is it?"

A few minutes passed before he spoke again. "I need you to…to touch me…before you see me."

I gave him a what-the-hell stare as my eyes widened

and my body reflexively pulled away. *"What?"* I asked, completely taken aback. "You want me to *touch* you? Alec, we literally just met…and I'm not ready for something like…"

"No!" He held up his hands to cut me off. "Nothing sexual, I swear. I just…I want you to touch my face…before you see me."

My shock shifted into confusion as my eyes narrowed in his direction. "But…why?"

He sighed as he took a step towards me. "Because I have to know…" he whispered.

"Know what?" I whispered back.

Our bodies were so close by that point that I could feel his chest rising and falling against mine.

He exhaled slowly, his warm breath escaping from the bottom of his mask, caressing my forehead. "I need to know if this is real."

His words were barely audible, but I knew exactly what he was referring to. The feelings between us had grown beyond anything either of us had ever expected. Falling for someone online doesn't always end with a 'happily ever after', so I could understand his apprehension. Though, I wasn't quite sure how touching him in any way whatsoever was going to prove if what we had was real.

"Please, Scarlett," he begged. There was an edge to his voice that I just could not shake.

"Okay," I agreed…but only because I didn't know what else to do.

When he extended his arms toward me, I could visibly see him trembling.

Instinctively, I reached out to hold both of his gloved hands in mine, offering him the same sort of stability he had given me when we first embraced.

"This is really difficult for me," he murmured.

"I can tell," I responded in a hushed tone. "What's going on?" I asked curiously.

He didn't reply. Instead, he turned his head to the side and removed his mask in a slow, calculated motion. In the dim light, I could barely see his profile, but I immediately noticed that something was off. His nose had a minor downward turn, making it look slightly too long for his face; and his chin seemed small and underdeveloped in comparison to the rest of his large manly frame.

As if he could feel my eyes on him, he took my hand and tugged me forward. I wasn't sure what to expect when he placed both of my palms on the sides of his face, but I heard his breathing increase exponentially.

He removed his hands from mine, leaving my fingers resting against his cheeks. In the same instant, his entire body went rigid, and a quiet whimper escaped his lips. He was clearly terrified of something, though I was still unsure of what.

"Touch me," he whispered painfully.

At first, I could not understand why this was such a big deal for him. I began to run my fingertips down his face, starting at his forehead, gently pushing back his long dark hair that kept falling into his eyes. I smiled as I trailed down the bridge of his nose, caressing his soft skin. But when my touch landed where his cheekbones should be, my brow furrowed.

Another tortured exhale left his lips as I rubbed my thumbs back and forth, trying to make sense of what I could not find.

"Look at me," I whispered.

His already-stiffened body stiffened further. "Scarlett, I…"

"Alec…" I breathed. "Look at me…please."

I watched his Adam's apple bob up and down as he swallowed nervously. His uncomfortable demeanor told me that he was not going to comply with my request, so I shifted my body until I was standing directly in front of him. When I placed my hand on his chest, his heart was beating so hard that I could feel it pulsing against my palm.

When I glanced up, a tiny gasp escaped my mouth before I could stop it. With the small amount of light reflecting off the diamond-tiered chandelier overhead, I was finally able to see Alec's entire face. The first thing I noticed were his eyes, which were currently squeezed shut. They were both slanted at a downward angle, and his lower eyelids seemed to droop. The strange positioning caused his brow and forehead to look slightly larger than they would have usually appeared. I reached up to touch his face once more, retracing my previous movements. The reason I couldn't feel his cheekbones was because he didn't have any, which was most likely the cause of his misshapen eyes.

Alec's whole body soon started trembling so hard that his teeth were chattering.

Without opening his eyes, he gracelessly moved his hair out of the way, revealing that he did not have any ears. At least, not what you or I would consider ears. Instead, there were two little, malformed nubs that seemed to curl in on themselves. Behind his right ear, I could see a glint of something silver.

"What is that?" I asked. I gently touched the small object in case he thought that I was referring to his lack of cartilage.

He cringed, but his eyes remained closed as he reluctantly responded. "It's the sound processor to my cochlear implant."

"So, you're...deaf?"

"No..." he breathed out painfully. "Not entirely."

A sad smile formed on my lips as I came to the realization that these abnormalities were the reason that he never wanted to send me pictures of himself...and why he didn't want to meet me in the first place.

"You're beautiful," I whispered.

His slanted eyes popped open, and he stared at me with an intensity that nearly took my breath away. Yet, the painful expression on his perfectly imperfect face nearly broke my heart.

I cupped his face in my hands and gently tugged him closer, forcing him to lean over at a slightly awkward angle. His brilliant baby-blues locked onto mine and I nearly lost myself in the deep cerulean pools. I stood on my tip-toes to kiss his forehead, then his cheeks, and lastly his lower jaw.

"You're beautiful," I said again.

Every muscle in his body seemed to tighten as he studied my expression, almost as if he didn't believe what had just come out of my mouth. No other words passed between us as he abruptly stood up straight again and slipped his mask back into place. Then he pulled me back out toward the party.

Neither of us said anything about his reveal for the rest of the evening...but I knew that once we were alone, we had much to discuss.

CHAPTER 10

The rest of the night played out like a dream. We ate dinner in a comfortable silence surrounded by my co-workers and friends. Though, unlike most of the men at our table, Alec chose to leave his mask in place; which meant that he had to move the bottom half away from his face to take each bite of his food.

Occasionally, we made eye contact and I would smile. His eyes crinkled in response, but even through the mask, I could tell that it was forced on his end.

From time to time, he would run his fingers through his long dark hair, allowing a glimpse of his ears to show. During the few times that he looked away, I tried to reimagine his features that were hiding underneath the mask, though I didn't dare stare for very long.

After our dinner, he ushered me back onto the dance floor and twirled me around as if we were the main attraction at the ball. Much to my surprise, he was a wonderful dancer...light on his feet and never faltering in his steps...unlike me, who kept stepping on his toes and scuffing up his recently polished shoes.

I quickly lost count of how many times that he grunted and groaned and laughed at my amateur dancing skills.

Eventually, he just picked me up to avoid further injury. The muscles in his arms tightened and flexed as he held me close against his firmly-toned torso.

The DJ shifted gears and chose that very moment to play 'Tubthumping' by Chumbawamba, which instantly turned the entire room full of costume-clad partygoers into a jumping, bouncing, screaming mosh pit.

I caught a brief glimpse of Liza as she crowd-surfed past me, shouting and cheering while attempting to sing along. But let's be honest, none of us really know all the words to that song. We just say blah-blah-blah-la-de-da until the chorus starts, and then we sing at the top of our lungs.

Then, as if fate knew we needed another slow song, 'Listen To Your Heart' by Roxette began to blare through the speakers, causing Alec and I to pause and stare at one another.

"Are you listening?" he whispered.

I grinned like an idiot as he took me back into his arms.

~*~*~*~

Nearing the end of the night, the DJ got on his microphone. "Alright, all you spooky ladies and frightening gents, it's nearly time for this terrifying evening to come to a close. And with the spirit of Halloween lingering in the air, there is only one way to say a final goodnight." A split second later, 'Thriller' by Michael Jackson began to play.

Now, I am not sure if what took place shortly thereafter was planned or not, but at least twenty people started lining up in the middle of the dance floor, twitching and stretching as if they were reenacting the movements in the music video.

And then suddenly, Alec disappeared from my side and joined in the lineup.

My eyes went wide, and a smile made its way across my face. *Is he seriously about to…?*

As the tempo of the song changed, the entire dance

group launched into the choreography routine as if they had been rehearsing together for weeks.

Alec's dazzling blue eyes stared straight at me while he nailed each move flawlessly.

I could not help myself as I started to clap and cheer and root them all on while my head bopped to the music.

Just before the song came to an end, Alec hobbled over to me as if he was a zombie and grabbed my arms to help me make the movements.

I giggled uncontrollably as I struggled to keep up.

Alec's eyes crinkled beneath his mask, a tell-tale sign that he was enjoying the moment.

When the song finally ended, the room burst into applause.

Alec wrapped his arm around my shoulder, so I slipped mine around his waist as we made our way to the exit.

"SCARLETT!" Liza's voice suddenly echoed from across the room.

I turned around and scanned the busy corridor.

She waved her hands in the air and jumped a few times to get my attention. "I'M GOING TO MEET UP WITH DEREK! SO JUST TAKE THE CAR, AND I'LL SEE YOU SOMETIME TOMORROW, OKAY?"

"YOU'RE STAYING THE NIGHT AT HIS PLACE?" I shouted back.

"YEP!" she returned.

"OKAY! HAVE FUN! LOVE YOU!" I called out.

Her voice echoed once more. "LOVE YOU MOST!"

~*~*~*~

Alec and I lingered at his car that just happened to be parked two spaces over from Liza's. I could tell that he had a lot running through his mind, though he didn't say a word.

A wave of courage swept over me as I finally asked the only question burning in my mind after everything that had transpired throughout the evening. "So, can we talk about earlier?"

"We will," he replied without missing a beat. "Tomorrow. I'll call you first thing in the morning."

I removed my mask and narrowed my eyes in his direction as the cars around us began to disperse. "No. Not tomorrow. Tonight. Right now, even."

Alec sighed. "Things are perfect right now. So, I don't want to ruin them by…" He finally looked my way as his words trailed off. His ice-blue eyes were shining through the dark mask as he stared at me in silence.

"What is it? What's wrong?" I finally asked.

"Nothing," he breathed. "Wow…" He reflexively reached out to caress my cheek. "You are…exquisite, Scarlett. The most beautiful woman I have ever laid eyes on." He let his hand fall away. "This…this is exactly why I want to wait…"

"Don't," I whispered. "Don't say anything else. Just follow me home." When he didn't respond, I placed my hand on his chest and added, "…please."

Alec sighed as his shoulders slumped momentarily. "Fine," he replied, though his tone suggested that he was less than thrilled about it.

CHAPTER 11

The whole way back to my house, I kept checking my rearview mirror to make sure that Alec was indeed behind me. My thought process was…if I can't see him, then he may try to get away…which was ridiculous, but I just could not seem to help it.

When I finally pulled into my driveway, I allowed myself to relax.

Alec parked right behind me and cut off his engine, but he stayed in his car. I strolled over to the driver's side door of his silver 69' Chevy Camaro. Both of his hands were gripping the steering wheel so tight that I could make out all the veins and tendons on each of his hands through the white gloves he was still wearing.

I gently tapped on the glass, half expecting him to roll down the window and offer up some excuse as to why he couldn't come inside…or perhaps he would tell me that he needed to leave. Instead, my light tapping seemed to shake him out of whatever trance he had been in.

He glanced up to meet my gaze as he released his hold on the steering wheel and opened the door.

When he stepped out, he glanced down at me. We were face to face once again…or in this case, face to mask. He still had not taken his off.

I eventually grabbed his hand and led him up the steps to my front porch. I only released my grip so that I could unlock the door. Then, I flipped on the light and gestured for him to come inside.

With Liza staying over at her boyfriend's house for their anniversary, Alec and I had the whole place to ourselves. And given what I briefly learned about him earlier, we definitely needed some time alone.

When I closed the door behind us and turned on more lights, Alec's posture seemed to tense up all over again. Almost instantly, he turned his back to me.

We had only known each other for about seven months through online chats and talking on the phone, but the level of comfort I had with this man was astounding. It was as if we had been in each other's lives forever; such a cliché, but it was honestly how I felt.

I wrapped my arms around his waist, linking my hands just above his belly button. Mostly because I wasn't sure what else I could do to ease his tormented mind.

I heard him sigh as he placed one of his hands on top of mine. "I feel like I'm in some live-action version of 'Beauty and the Beast,'" he said sadly.

I sighed quietly. "This isn't a movie, Alec. And you are no beast." Already knowing that he wasn't going to turn around, I shifted my body to where I was standing in front of him with my arms still around his waist.

He sighed deeply as he wrapped his arms around my shoulders. "I know this must seem quite childish for me to be acting this way, but…"

"No," I interrupted. "Nothing about this is childish."

He hugged me a little tighter; then he laughed softly. "I swear…I'm not usually like this…so uptight and self-conscious."

I glanced up, and we locked eyes.

Alec was shaking his head as another laugh escaped. "I promise you that this isn't the real me," he finished.

I swallowed down my nerves. "So...let me see *you* then," I said bravely.

Alec took a small step back, slipping out of my embrace. Slowly and meticulously, he began to remove the gloves from his hands. First, the left; then, the right. Then he gestured toward the living room. "Can we sit down?"

"Sure," I replied casually.

He followed me through the small archway. And a few seconds later, we were sitting side by side on the loveseat.

He swallowed hard as he cleared his throat and turned to look at me. "I guess I should start with the most obvious thing...I was born with what is called, Treacher Collins Syndrome. It's basically a condition that affects the bones and tissues of my face." He touched his mask as if to make sure it was still there. "Anyway," he cleared his throat again and placed his gloves beside him. "The only thing I know for sure is that my birth mother was a fifteen-year-old runaway...which was far too young to be caring for a baby, especially one with special needs. I was told that she gave me up for adoption shortly after I was born," he paused and leaned forward, reaching into his back pocket, "...but not before she said a proper goodbye." He opened his black leather wallet and handed me a faded Polaroid photograph. "Very few people in my life have seen this."

I studied the grainy image of a young girl holding a tiny baby wrapped in a blue blanket. Her eyes were closed in a peaceful expression, and she was gently kissing him on the forehead. "This is beautiful."

Alec met my gaze through the mask and placed his hand on my knee, then his eyes crinkled, revealing a smile. "Giving me up was probably the best thing she could have ever done for me, though I'm sure it was very difficult for her. But my parents are the most amazing people in the entire world. They adopted me when I was just three-weeks-old. My older sister, Cora, used to call me her 'special little china doll' because my face looked so delicate."

I returned his smile. "That's very sweet."

"My family is wonderful, and they've done everything they could to give me everything I would ever want or need…but growing up with TCS wasn't easy. When I was young, I never really cared that I looked different from other kids my age. My mom and dad always told me that I was special. That I was perfect just the way I was. That I was unique. But it wasn't until middle school when I realized that being unique isn't always accepted."

I watched his eyes grow distant as he stared past me while he continued.

"I was extremely thin at that age, and I had had a growth spurt over the summer, so I was called 'beanpole' quite often. That didn't bother me much, though. But then a group of kids started making fun of my ears, calling me 'nubby'. Or they'd point at my face and call me Frankenstein." He paused and sighed again. "I've had more surgeries than I can count…starting when I was very young. Some were to help with my hearing, others…well, they were supposed to give my face a more natural look. But I knew that I would never have normal features. Not by society's standards anyway. So, I stopped trying to physically change myself."

I reached out to run my fingers through his hair. "Normal is overrated," I said quietly.

He sighed once more and closed his eyes at my touch.

"I want to see you."

He instantly covered the mask with his hand. "Not yet," he replied softly. "I couldn't bear…" His words trailed off as a pained expression took over what little bit I could see of his face.

"Tell me what you're afraid of," I urged him. "Do you think I'm going to tell you to leave? That I'll run away and lock myself in my room to get away from you?"

He pulled away and shifted his entire body uncomfortably.

"Alec," I whispered sternly. "You're still the same man I met online. The same man that I've been IM'ing with every night for over seven months. The same man whose voice is the last sound I want to hear in this world before I fall asleep each night..."

"I'm afraid to lose all that," he admitted quietly.

With a burst of courage, I blurted out, "If you honestly think that some external flaws on your body are going to make me turn away from you, then you really don't know me at all. And honestly, I'm a bit offended that you'd think me so shallow."

He scoffed, and his eyes widened with surprise.

I sighed and reached for his hand, giving it a little squeeze. "Take off the mask," I pleaded.

In the bright lights of my living room, I could fully see the distress in his body posture as he continued with his internal struggle.

"Alec," I paused and held his alarmed stare. "I've already seen a glimpse...and I think you're perfect just the way you are."

Because of his brief reveal earlier in the evening, I was semi-prepared for what I was about to see. But his trembling hands stopped me from pushing him any further.

"Okay," I breathed. "It's okay. You don't have to."

"I know I don't have to...I need to. This shouldn't be so damn hard for me..."

Much to my surprise, he let out a shaky breath as he reached for the ribbon at the back of his head. His fingers fumbled slightly as he gently pulled, releasing the little bow. His Adam's apple bobbed again as he finally lowered the mask into his lap, but he kept his face angled down for the next few minutes.

When he eventually looked my way, I could not help

but smile. He was even more handsome than I could have ever imagined.

Dazzling sky-blue eyes stared back at me through thick upper lashes. The unusual physical characteristics of his face were most definitely noticeable, though they could not take away from his undeniably attractive features. His jawline was clenched as if he could not stand being under my scrutinizing gaze.

Then, before I could stop myself, I ended up in his lap with my mouth pressed firmly against his. His lips were as smooth as silk and soft like velvet. The course stubble on his lower jaw scratched my skin, but I didn't care.

It took me a few seconds to realize that he wasn't interacting with me. In fact, he had not moved at all. I pulled away to look at him, but the instant our eyes locked, he pulled me back toward him.

His arms wrapped around me, holding me firmly against his upper body. I sighed against his mouth just before he slipped his tongue past my lips, causing a shiver to run down the full length of my spine.

His kiss was the most passionate thing I had ever experienced in my entire twenty-four years.

Everything inside me was on fire...tingling from my head to my toes...like a blissful, euphoric high coursing through my veins and engulfing my soul in lustful flames. My heart was beating wildly, and my mind was consumed with every detail that had led up to that moment.

Without breaking away, Alec meticulously removed his perfectly-tailored tuxedo jacket and tossed it onto the floor.

A split second later, as if the universe had waited for that very moment to interrupt, there was a commotion at the front door.

Liza's angry voice drifted through the kitchen. "I have had..." The door slammed shut. "...the worse night of my damn life!" Her keys and purse clattered onto the counter. "I ended up having to take a cab to the restaurant because

Derek never showed to pick me up! And by the time I got there, he was already plastered-ass-drunk!" Her high-heeled stilettos hit the floor one clunk at a time. "Apparently, he had been out celebrating long before our date. So much for our two-year anniversary!" She growled and sighed. "I mean, seriously...how messed up is thaaaa...?" Liza abruptly stopped talking the moment she appeared in the living room.

I slid off of Alec's lap as casually as possible. Almost immediately, he angled his head down and covered his face with his hands.

"Oh, my gosh!" Liza squealed with delight. "Is this Alec?" And just like that, her horrible night with Derek was forgotten.

I felt myself smile as I placed my hand on Alec's thigh. "Indeed, it is." I lowered my voice to a whisper so that only he could hear me. "Would you like to meet my best friend?"

Before Alec had a chance to respond, Liza had taken it upon herself to get overly friendly. "It's so nice to finally meet you!" she gushed. "Scarlett talks about you all the time!" She extended her hand, waiting for a handshake. "Well, I mean...not *all* the time...but like...ya know...a normal amount..."

In the midst of her rambling, Alec stood to his full height in one fluid motion, then he cleared his throat and placed his hand in hers. "Nice to meet you, too," he replied.

Liza's brow furrowed as if she was trying to decipher something, but she wasn't quite sure what.

Alec's expression was twisted somewhere between fear and anger as the two of them stared at each other for a rather uncomfortable amount of time.

I cleared my throat to get Liza's attention. Which seemed to do the trick as she dropped Alec's hand and focused her gaze on me.

I raised my eyebrow. "Can you give us a minute alone?"

"Oh...right...I'm, uh...sorry," she stammered. "You

two have fun." Then she offered a small smile before she disappeared down the hall toward her bedroom.

Alec was still standing in the exact spot he was in when my best friend walked away, but his shoulders seemed to be rising and falling in a rather distressed manner.

"I'm sorry about Liza," I said softly. "She's not usually so awkward around new people."

"She stared at me like I was some kind of freak!" he seethed.

I shook my head, "No. That's not it at all! She just wasn't expecting you to look...different."

His gaze landed on me, angry and clearly pissed-off. "Look different, eh? That's all? So now the truth comes out! You think I'm just some side-show-display that you can parade around? Giving false sympathy to my face, then you'll turn right around and criticize me behind my back? Is that the type of person you are, Scarlett?" He lumbered toward me, towering over me with a vicious demeanor that I would never have believed him capable of. "I should have expected it. After all, I've encountered that type of shit my whole life." He paused and scowled while shaking his head. "Well, you know what? Screw this! Screw this whole thing!" He gestured between us. "You can take all your pathetic compliments and your pitiful stares and..."

"*WHAT?*" I shouted in utter disbelief, cutting him off. I took a couple steps backward, mostly from shock, but also because he was quite scary when he was mad. "I never said anything like that! Nor would I ever think that way about you. All I said was that you look different! Because you do! We all do!"

He grabbed his jacket and shrugged it back on without giving me a second glance.

I tried again to calm him down. "Alec, all I'm saying is that everyone is different; from skin color to eye color, hair color, freckles, glasses, short, tall..."

"STOP!" he fumed. "Just...stop! I knew this was a

mistake." Without another word, he stormed past me so fast that I could feel a breeze from his body. Then he threw open the front door and disappeared into the moonlit night.

I followed him outside and chased him down the steps while calling his name the whole time, but he never acknowledged me.

He didn't stop walking, and he didn't look back. He just got in his car and peeled out of my driveway, heading toward town.

In a panicked state of unwanted desperation, I rushed back inside to grab my keys. I called out to Liza that I would be back, and then I hopped in my car and sped down the road.

A few streets over I finally caught up to Alec at a red light. He turned left, heading for the interstate. So, I followed close behind.

A little over an hour later, he got off the main highway, taking exit twenty-one. I tried to stay as close as possible without being too obvious. I didn't know the area very well, and with it being nighttime, if I lost sight of his car I would have no choice other than to turn around and head back home.

He drove straight for a few more minutes before making a quick right turn into an apartment complex. I hovered at the entrance while I watched him pull into one of the parking spaces. My engine idled as he walked up a small flight of stairs to the second floor. Then he fumbled with his keys, before unlocking the door and heading inside. Once I saw a light switch on, I quickly pulled into the parking space next to his car.

I cut off the engine and sat there for a few minutes. Mostly debating what the hell I was going to say when I approached him. *Would he flip out on me for following him home? Would he lash out and call me some crazy stalker? Or...would he apologize and invite me inside to talk about things like a rational adult?* I sighed heavily. I hated not knowing what to expect. It was like I had to continuously walk on eggshells for this man.

I was just about to get out of my car when Alec suddenly reappeared in his doorway, holding a leash. A large German Shepard followed him down the steps and onto the sidewalk. I slid down in my seat so he wouldn't be able to see me, silently cursing my leather interior for being so damn noisy as it squeaked in protest.

Alec ushered Sarge toward the end of the block and disappeared around the corner. I debated whether or not I should stay put or wait for him on the steps, but in the end, I decided to stay where I was...slouched down uncomfortably in my seat.

About fifteen minutes later, Alec and Sarge came sauntering back into my line of sight. With my hand hovering near the handle, I waited until they were almost directly in front of my car before I opened my door.

"Alec..." I said softly.

His head snapped up and his body tensed as his gaze landed on mine. I could hear Sarge growling by his side, but Alec simply pat the dog on the head and said, "It's okay, boy."

Instantly, Sarge responded by snorting and sitting down beside his master, watching me curiously with his head cocked to the side.

I stood there silently, shifting my weight from one foot to the other while practically hiding behind my driver's side door.

"You followed me home," Alec stated.

"Great observation," I replied quickly. I wasn't sure how my sarcastic response was going to be received, especially given the circumstances that led me there. But much to my surprise, he smirked.

He relaxed his posture and gestured with his head toward the second floor. "Would you like to come in?"

I nodded. "If you don't mind."

CHAPTER 12

I stood awkwardly in Alec's small foyer while he unhooked Sarge's leash. The dog instantly rushed to his bed nearby and began to chew on a rawhide bone.

Alec slowly turned around to face me. The tails of his tuxedo looked like a temporary superhero cape as they came to rest against the back of his legs. He stretched his arm past me to close the door. "I still can't believe you followed me home," he said humorously.

"I thought you were going to be angry," I replied. "Maybe yell at me again…or worse." In that moment, I realized how crazy my actions had been. Running after him without really knowing what I could have been running into.

Alec's smile instantly faded. "I would never hurt you, Scarlett. The way I reacted earlier…I just…" He sighed. "The way your friend looked at me…I got those stares all my life…and they were usually followed by taunts…or violence. I forgot myself for a moment."

I nodded. "I get that, Alec…but it still made me a little nervous."

"Well, something deep inside your heart told you that you

could trust me, or you wouldn't be here right now. Right?"

I smiled then and looked shyly at the ground. "You got me there."

"Look," he sighed again, "I know I must seem like some scared, insecure, little boy that can't keep his temper in check…but I swear to God, that isn't who I am. I mean, sure, I used to be that way. I used to lash out at anyone that ever stared at me for too long, but I've grown up. I accepted who I am a long time ago." He laughed half-heartedly. "If my friends would have seen how I've been acting the last couple days, they'd be like, 'Alec, what the hell is wrong with you? Have you gone crazy?'" He sighed once more as his smile faltered. "It's just…with you…I feel like I've found something that I didn't even realize I was looking for. The man you see in front of you right now…the man who spent the entire evening in your arms…the man who constantly drives you crazy with his annoying ways…" He paused as his smile slowly returned. "…*that* is who I really am. I may be an asshole sometimes…" His smile widened. "I won't deny that, but I'm not the angry person I once was. You…you make me a better version of myself. You make me so damn happy. I'm just…" He hesitated for half a second before taking my hand and pulling me in for a hug. "I'm trying to say that I care for you very deeply, and I'm sorry. Those words may not be enough to make up for how I ran out on you, but I truly am sorry. And it won't happen again, I promise."

My arms found their way around his waist as I leaned my head against his chest. His heart started to beat out of control as I gazed up into his beautiful blue eyes.

He caressed my cheek with his fingertips just before he tenderly cupped my face in his hands and leaned down. "Never again will I scare you, and never again will I make you doubt me."

Everything leading up to that moment had me on such an emotional rollercoaster that I was unable to think straight.

My mind kept circling, thinking about all the months that I had begged to meet him, and all the times he had turned me down.

I smiled involuntarily as I recalled the moment when he finally said yes. Then I closed my eyes as I began to relive our wonderful time at the ball...finally getting to see him face to face, and understanding the reasons for all his crazy behavior...finally getting to feel the tenderness of our first kiss, only to watch him flee in anger a short while later.

Alec brought me back to my senses when he whispered, "I feel like I've been waiting my whole life for you." Then he pressed his velvety lips to mine for the second time.

My entire body responded to his touch as if I had experienced it hundreds of times before.

Alec removed his jacket again without breaking our kiss, tossing it aside. His hands gently gripped the back of my head, tugging me closer.

Before I could stop myself, my fingers were releasing the buttons on his dress shirt one by one, revealing his flawlessly tan skin.

Alec moaned quietly against my mouth as he helped me to remove his shirt from his broad shoulders.

I pulled away from him long enough to notice that his entire left arm, from shoulder to wrist, was completely covered in stunning designs. I gasped in awe as I reached out to touch his beautifully decorated skin.

From his shoulder to his elbow was an extraordinary image of a galaxy that wrapped around his muscular upper arm. Perfectly placed stars seemed to light up the blue and purple ink as they swirled together, blending into the yellow and orange closer to the center. I ran my fingers over the star-strewn sky until the picture suddenly changed. The bottom half of his arm, from his elbow to his wrist, was covered in smoke and fire. In the midst of the chaos, was an arm reaching upward toward the peaceful night sky. I squinted my eyes and took a closer look. Written on the forearm were three words: Strength. Faith. Overcome.

My gaze eventually made its way back to his face. "Wow," I blurted out. "This is amazing! Is there a meaning behind it?"

He tenderly ran his fingers over the whole design, stopping at the outstretched hand. "My mom used to tell me, 'To have the strength to overcome life's obstacles, you first must have faith that something better is just around the corner.'" He stared into my eyes intensely. "I know now how true that statement is…because I found you."

Before I had the chance to say anything, Alec's arms were around me again, and his mouth was back against my lips. "I need you, Scarlett," he said hungrily.

The ribbons on my corset were gently pulled away, and the zipper was slid down, causing my dress to pool on the floor at my feet.

Alec then traced his fingertips up and down my back while his tongue danced with mine.

My hands wandered all over his sculpted upper body, feeling every dip and bulge of his lean muscular frame. "This is going too fast," I whispered through kisses.

"Yes, it is," he agreed. His fingers gently raked through my hair. "Do you want me to stop?"

I glanced up at his desire-filled stare as I ran my thumb over his bottom lip. "No."

He smiled seductively. "Good." The next thing I knew, he was effortlessly lifting me off the floor, cradling me against his body, and taking me down a darkened hallway.

My mind was screaming at me to slow down, but my body did not seem to care. All the feelings and desires that had been developing between us over the last few months seemed to overflow all at once.

Alec's kisses soon became desperate and wild as he laid me down on his bed…his hands roaming freely…clothing disappearing.

"Is this okay?" he asked breathlessly.

I gently pulled his body on top of mine and wrapped my legs around his waist. "Yes," I whispered back.

"I want you, Scarlett…I want you more than I have ever wanted anything in my entire life…"

My next three words came out without a second thought. "Then take me."

His face was hovering just centimeters above mine. "Are you sure?"

I nodded eagerly, biting my lip. "I'm sure."

A slow smile spread across his face as he eased his body into position.

A rush of air expelled from my mouth as we suddenly became one.

Alec took his time, moving slowly and tenderly; devouring every inch of me as if he could not seem to get enough.

The words that he whispered in my ear took my breath away as our bodies entwined and our souls merged.

In that moment, there was nothing and no one else in this world.

Only Alec…only me…only us.

CHAPTER 13

The next morning, I woke up in a pair of Alec's boxers and one of his oversized t-shirts. I still could not believe that I had stayed the night, let alone given myself to him so freely.

I blew out my breath slowly as I turned over to see Alec sleeping soundly beside me. A smile crept across my lips as I reached over to move a few strands of hair from his face.

He immediately stirred, and his beautiful blue eyes fluttered open. When his gaze landed on me, he grinned sleepily. "Good morning, beautiful."

I giggled at his groggy tone. "Good morning."

He moaned softly as he stretched out his arms and legs, elongating his entire body beneath the covers, before propping himself up on his elbow and staring in my direction. "Did you sleep well?"

I blushed under his sleepy, lustful stare. "Yeah, I did. What about you?"

His grin widened. "Most definitely." Then he practically lunged at me and placed both hands on either side of my head. His long dark hair tickled my cheeks as he leaned down and kissed me gently on the tip of my nose. "Want some breakfast?"

I could not stop myself from laughing at the adorable look on his face. "I'd love some."

He kissed my nose again. "As you wish."

I bit my lip as my smile grew wider. "Quoting from my favorite movie now, eh?"

He flashed me his perfect smile. "You can be my Buttercup…and I'll be your Westley." Then he stood up and headed for his bedroom door.

"ALEC!" I shouted through laughter. "Where are your clothes?"

He turned around with an innocent expression. "On you." Then he smirked before walking away.

I covered my face with his blanket to hide my red cheeks.

A few minutes later, I heard him clanking around in the kitchen. "SCRAMBLED OR OVER-EASY?" he called out.

I chuckled to myself. "SCRAMBLED PLEASE."

"AS YOU WISH."

I heard cabinets and drawers opening and closing, then a few more clanking sounds.

I had to see what was going on in there.

I climbed out of Alec's comfortable bed and made my way down the hallway. Sarge greeted me by wagging his tail, causing a thump-thump-thump against the floor.

"Can't sneak up on me with him around," Alec called out with a chuckle.

"Clearly not," I replied.

I strolled into the kitchen and found Alec standing in front of the stove…completely naked…with only an apron to cover the front of his body.

When he turned around, I nearly lost my composure. The top of the apron said, *May I Suggest The Sausage*, and had an arrow pointing down.

With a spatula in one hand and a plate in the other, Alec said, "Now before you say anything about this…it was a gag-gift from my best friend for my birthday last year. He's a bit, um…immature; more like what people would call a man-child."

I had to cover my mouth to stop myself from bursting. "Uh huh, whatever you say," I muttered sarcastically.

He smirked again as he busied himself with making our breakfast. "It's the only apron I have, okay?"

"I'm not complaining," I told him teasingly.

A short while later, after Alec put some clothes on, we ate a delicious breakfast of eggs, toast, and orange juice.

"So," he said as he took a bite of toast, "I'd like to take you out today. Maybe show you some of the places where I grew up."

I smiled as I placed my glass back onto the table. "I'd like that. But..."

He paused with his fork halfway to his mouth. "But what?"

I raised one of my eyebrows. "*But* the only clothes I have are my dress from the Halloween Ball…and what I'm currently wearing right now. Definitely not something I'd want to wear out in public."

His fork full of eggs finally made it past his smiling lips. "I think some of my sister's clothes are still in a box in my closet…they got mixed in with mine when I moved. But I'm sure some of them will fit you."

~*~*~*~

After rifling through a box shoved into the far corner of Alec's closet, I made my way to the living room in a pair of faded, ripped-up jeans and a Backstreet Boys t-shirt.

Alec was sitting on the couch in a pair of dark blue jeans and a tight white t-shirt lacing up his sneakers. He glanced my way and smirked. "Nice choice."

I playfully rolled my eyes. "Hey, don't knock my boys!"

Alec laughed and then started singing, "*Although loneliness has always been a friend of mine, I'm leaving my life in your hands...*" He stood and took a step toward me. "*People say I'm crazy and that I am blind, riskin' it all in a glance...*" He pulled me against his body and wrapped his arms around me as he continued singing. *"And how you've got me blind is still a mystery. I can't get you outta my head...don't care what is written in your history...as long as you're here with me...*" He hit every single note flawlessly as he took my hand and spun me around.

I could not help but sing along with him. *"I don't care who you are...where you're from...what you did...as long as you love me."*

Alec grinned and kissed my forehead before calling Sarge over. "Gonna take him for a quick walk; then we can head out."

"Sounds good," I replied. "I just need to brush my teeth, and then I'm good to go. Do you have an extra...?"

He answered before I had even finished my sentence. "In the cabinet under the sink. There should be a new pack."

I chuckled. "Thanks."

~*~*~*~

Twenty minutes later, Alec and I were cruising down the highway with the windows down and the radio on low.

I watched him from the corner of my eye. The wind whipped through his hair, causing the thick tendrils to swirl and caress his ruggedly handsome face. His body posture was calm and in control, with one hand on the steering wheel and the other propped up on the opened window. The sun was gleaming off the colorful designs of his tattoos, making them seem even more vivid and bright.

I only tore my eyes away from him when a familiar guitar riff caught my attention.

"Do you mind if I turn this up?" I asked, glancing back in his direction.

He smiled without taking his eyes off the road. "Go for it."

I reached for the volume and slowly turned the knob until 'Photograph' by Def Leppard was blaring through the speakers. I smiled to myself as I stuck my arm out the window, making little wave-like motions, letting the strong breeze tug my hand back and forth.

With the last verse fading, I turned the volume back down. "I just love that song."

"Me, too," Alec replied.

Vehicles and scenery passed by in a blur as I listened to the hum of Alec's Camaro's engine that was nearly drowning out the music playing faintly in the background.

Thirty to forty-five minutes later, we finally got off the interstate and started driving on some winding back roads in the midst of the mountainous countryside.

Alec slowed to a crawl and turned onto an unmarked dirt road.

"Where are we going exactly?"

He bit his lip and smiled. "You'll see. We're almost there."

A few minutes later, we stopped in front of a huge, grey, stone wall with an oversized wooden gate.

I cast Alec a questioning stare, but he didn't look my way. Instead, he put the car into park, got out, pressed a few numbers into a keypad on the wall, and then got back behind the wheel. A split second later, the gates opened inward and Alec pulled on through.

We slowly made our way around a long curving driveway that eventually led us to an elegant, two-story, multicolored-stone mansion. The windows were each framed in a dark chocolate trim, matching the oversized double doors at the front of the house.

Expertly cut shrubbery lined the walkway that connected the driveway to the front porch. And a three-tiered fountain, completely surrounded by pink and yellow flowers, sat in the middle of a perfectly manicured lawn. The grass was such a vibrant shade of green that it almost looked like a plush velvet rug.

Alec casually pulled up to one of the three-car garage doors and pressed a button on his keychain. The sleek wooden door slowly lifted, allowing Alec to park inside.

When he cut off the engine, I turned my entire body toward him. "Okay…seriously…where the hell are we?"

I could have sworn I saw a twinkle in his eye when he responded, "I thought you might like to meet my family today."

CHAPTER 14

My heart was pounding as Alec took my hand and led me up the walkway. "I wish you would have told me where we were going," I stated in an irritated tone as I attempted to fix my messy hair. "I would have picked a different outfit."

"You look amazing," he told me.

I gave him a sideways glare. "I look like a fan-girl."

He smirked. "Aren't you, though?"

I smacked him playfully. "Not the impression I wanted to give your family..."

Suddenly the double doors opened, and a beautiful woman in her late sixties with shoulder-length blonde hair rushed forward. "Alec!" she gushed. Then she wrapped her arms around him for a tight embrace.

Alec chuckled and returned the hug. "Hi, mom."

She released him and took a step back. "I didn't know you were coming by today. What a pleasant surprise!" Then she noticed me and smiled, "Well, hello there." She turned back to her son. "And who is your lovely friend?"

Alec casually draped his arm around my shoulder. "This is Scarlett...the girl I've been telling you about." He looked at me and grinned. "Scarlett...this is my mom, Lindy."

He has been telling her about me? My heart pitter-pattered happily inside my chest as I smiled and extended my hand, "Nice to meet you."

But Alec's mother just stared at my open palm as if it was the strangest gesture she had ever seen. "No, no, dear...no hand-shaking in this house." Then without any warning, she pulled me in for a tight hug. "This is how to greet the people we care about."

I chuckled lightly and returned her embrace. "I'll have to remember that for next time."

She released me and smiled. "Good to hear." Then she linked her arm with mine and ushered me inside. She called over her shoulder, "C'mon, Alec...you might as well come, too. No use in you standing on the front porch all day."

I heard Alec laugh behind me as he closed the door.

When we stepped into the foyer, a quiet gasp escaped my lips. The luxurious room was encased in white from floor to ceiling...and was bigger than my entire condo.

Straight ahead, a large diamond-tiered chandelier hung directly in the center of two massive staircases, each one curving slightly as they led up to the second floor. Black-iron railings with curling vine designs extended the full length of each staircase, as well as the entire upper level.

"Whoa..." My whisper seemed to echo throughout the room, bouncing off the shiny grey and white marble floors, and then disappearing through the circular sunroof overhead.

Alec's mother led me past the double staircases and into a spacious sunroom with brilliant rays of light pouring in from every direction, enveloping us in the sun's warmth. Two grey suede sofas, both in the shape of crescent moons, faced each other with an oversized glass coffee table directly in the center. A stone fireplace sat on the back wall, which was the only part of the room that didn't have a window. Just outside was a small balcony that overlooked a seemingly endless lake with the ever-expanding mountain range rising behind it. The rolling hills reflected off the water, giving the illusion of two worlds in one.

I sat down beside Lindy, and she gestured for Alec to sit directly across from us.

She smiled at me and clasped her hands on top of mine. "So, how does it feel to finally meet in person after so long of talking on the interwebs?"

I glanced at Alec.

He smiled lovingly in his mother's direction. "Inter-NET, mom," he corrected her.

She waved his words away. "Web...net...close enough for me."

I laughed. "It's pretty amazing to finally see his face. He kept me waiting long enough."

"Oh, really?" She looked in Alec's direction. "It's not gentleman-like to keep a lady waiting. I thought your father and I had taught you better than that."

I bit my lip to stop my smile from reaching its full capacity. "Yeah, *Alec*...so rude."

Lindy started to laugh.

Alec decided to redirect the conversation away from himself. "So, mom...did you happen to notice anything special about the shirt that Scarlett is wearing?"

Lindy gently tugged on my shoulder as she leaned forward to get a better look. "Oh!" she exclaimed. "Cora, Alec's sister, used to have a shirt exactly like that! She wore it all the time! What are the odds?"

"What are the odds, indeed?" Alec grinned deviously in my direction.

The front door suddenly opened and closed. "Lindy, darling...I'm home!"

"In the sunroom, my love! We have visitors!" she called back.

The sound of footsteps got closer until Alec's father appeared in the archway. A smile broke out across his face when his gaze landed on his son.

Alec stood and nimbly hopped over the back of the couch. "Hey, dad!"

The two men embraced in a bear-hug, slapping each other on the back. "It's so good to see you, son! What brings you by today?"

Alec gestured for me to come over to him. "There's someone very special I wanted you and mom to meet."

Just like before, Alec wrapped his arm around my shoulder. "Scarlett, this is my dad...Henry."

Alec's father's big brown eyes suddenly widened, and he smiled. "Ah, so this is the young lady that we've heard so much about! A pleasure to finally meet you, my dear."

I could not stop myself from blushing. "Nice to meet you, too."

Because of Lindy's warning only moments ago, I was fully prepared when Henry scooped me up off the floor for a squeeze-hug.

A short while later, all four of us were sitting on the balcony, chatting and laughing while staring out at the serene landscape surrounding us.

"Wanna go swimming?" Alec randomly blurted out.

"I don't have a suit," I replied quickly.

"I'm sure you could borrow one of Cora's," Lindy offered. "She's got plenty."

Alec grinned. "What a great idea, mom!"

I shook my head. That man was incorrigible.

"C'mon," Alec said as he took my hand.

I followed him inside and up the stairs, passing by frame after frame of family photographs. I stopped to linger at a few, running my fingers tenderly over Alec's face in each one. "You were such a cute little boy."

He spun around, looking highly offended. "Am I not cute now?"

Laughter was the only reply I was able to give in response to the look on his face. "You are definitely still a cutie-pie."

Alec feigned irritation. "Ohhh...now you're just mocking me!"

I placed my hand on my chest and faked a gasp. "I would never!"

He smiled and pulled me in for a quick hug. "Wait here," he told me. "I'll get a few suits from Cora's closet so you can try them on."

I lingered in the hallway as he disappeared into the last room on the left. When he returned, he had three different suits in his hand. As he gave them to me, I noticed that they all still had the price tags on them.

"Uh, these are brand new, Alec."

He raised an eyebrow. "So?"

I rolled my eyes. "*So*, that means she must have recently bought them...for herself. Shouldn't she be the first to wear them?"

Alec copied my eye roll. "My sister has like thirty different bathing suits in there. I really don't think she'll care if you wear *one* of them."

"You're sure?"

He nodded. "It'll be fine. The bathroom is right there." He pointed to the door behind me. "I'll be across the hall in my old room. I'm sure I've still got a pair of shorts in there somewhere." He kissed the top of my head before he walked away.

I entered the bathroom and stared at the suits. Light blue. Neon pink. And black. Those were the choices Alec had picked for me. I scoffed at the slinky pink one that reminded me of the character Leeloo in the movie 'The Fifth Element'. *Nope...not gonna happen...sorry, Alec.*

So, I tried on the blue one. Everything seemed fine until I checked out the back. I let out a chuckle. Way too much of my bottom was showing. *Next...*

I sighed as I tried on the last choice. I braced myself for another disappointment before glancing in the mirror. *Hmm...well, whatta-ya-know, this one fits perfectly. All the right places are covered, and all the right assets are showing. We have a winner!*

I hung the other two bathing suits on the back of the bathroom door before I gathered up my clothes...well, Cora's clothes...then I reached for the handle.

The collision happened before either of us had a chance to react.

I immediately recognized her face from the pictures in the hallway. Cora. Her long, dark, curly hair fell over her shoulders in waves. And her big brown eyes were staring at me with a shocked expression, which quickly turned to anger.

"What the hell...?" she blurted out. "Are those my...?"

Thankfully, Alec appeared behind us, wearing only a pair of red board shorts. "Well hey, sis! I didn't know you would be coming to visit the 'rents today. How are...?"

Cora turned her attention to her brother. "Alec! Are you fucking kidding me? How many times have I told you not to let your skanky female friends wear my stuff?! I thought you were over this playboy partying bullshit!" Her angry glare then shifted back to me as she looked me up and down. "You can keep the damn suit. I didn't like that one anyway." Then she walked away in a huff.

Alec looked stunned for about half of a second. "Whoa, Cora! Hold up! It's not like that!" he called after her. He jogged down the hall, leaving me standing on my own, in complete shock and embarrassment.

I watched the two of them arguing at the top of the landing. Cora was pointing in my direction with a pissed-off look on her face. Alec then threw his arms in the air and shook his head from side to side. Cora's hands instantly went to her hips as she stared at him with an angry scowl, then she poked his chest a few times and said something through gritted teeth before turning on her heel and disappearing down the stairs.

Alec's shoulders rose and fell as if he was taking a slow

deep breath; then he started walking back in my direction.

Skanky female friends? A playboy? I could not stop my hands from trembling by the time he made it back in front of me.

"I'm so sorry, Scarlett. I didn't think she was going to… I just…" He sighed.

"What the hell was that about, Alec?" I clutched the clothes in my hands closer to my chest.

"It's a complete misunderstanding."

I eyed him skeptically. "Didn't seem like it."

"ALEC? SCARLETT?" Lindy's voice interrupted our brief conversation. "IS EVERYTHING OKAY?"

"YES, MOM," Alec called back. "BE DOWN IN A MINUTE!"

More than a minute passed, and Alec and I still had not moved.

Eventually, soft footsteps came up the stairs, and his mother appeared on the top landing. "What's going on?" She looked back and forth between us. "You sure everything is alright?"

"We're fine, mom. Cora, just…she said some things to Scarlett that…"

"What sort of things?" Lindy interrupted.

"I think she was upset that I was wearing her new suit. I want to apologize, but…"

Lindy's brow furrowed. "That doesn't sound like Cora at all!" She placed her hand gently on my shoulder. "I'll talk to her."

"No, that's okay, I'll just…"

Alec cut me off. "We'll handle it, mom. It's got nothing to do with Scarlett. Cora is angry at me."

Lindy's concerned gaze became solely fixed on her son. "What are you two fighting about now?"

"It's nothing recent…it's an old situation that was apparently never resolved."

Lindy raised an eyebrow and gave him a look that only a

mother could give. "Whatever it is, you two better fix it! You're both adults; petty bickering is for children."

Alec sighed. "I know. We will."

Her expression didn't change.

Alec chuckled. "I promise, mom...damn!"

She smiled then. "That's all I wanted to hear."

CHAPTER 15

Alec and I walked side by side down the short wooden dock that was floating on the lake. I desperately wanted to talk about what had happened with his sister. I wanted to know what she meant by all those things she said, but his body language told me that was a bad idea.

When we reached the end of the dock, he didn't even hesitate as he dove in head first. The water was so clear that I could see his magnificent body gliding smoothly beneath the surface.

When he came up for a breath, he swam back to the dock and propped his arms up on the edge near my feet. His dark hair fell into his face as he looked up at me with his smoldering gaze. "Join me?"

Any other time, the sweet tone of his voice and the sight of his perfect smile would have been enough to make me melt into a puddle and dive right into his arms, but right then, all I could think about was what had taken place upstairs. The things Cora said about him, none of it made any sense…and it definitely did not sound like the Alec I had come to know.

In one graceful motion, Alec lifted himself out of the water and back onto dry land. A small waterfall cascaded down his body as he stood to his full height. Then he reached out to touch my chin with his fingertips before tilting my head up. When our eyes met, his expression changed. "Everything you're wondering about right now…everything that's circling around in your mind…I promise I will explain all of it." He sighed and shook his head slightly. "Right now, I just want you to be with me in this moment." He paused to move a piece of my hair behind my ear. "You've met my family; you've seen where I grew up…so, now you have a bit more insight as to who I am and where I come from…" He sighed again. "The person I used to be, I can't change him…I can't go back and undo any of the stupid shit I've done…"

Then it was my turn to sigh. "I'm not asking you to delete your past, Alec. But it's a little difficult to just brush aside what happened in there. I don't understand…"

His gentle touch remained on my face as he nodded slowly. "Okay…" he whispered. "You're right. I owe you an explanation about that, but…"

"No 'buts'…just tell me the truth. That's all I want to hear."

Alec blew out his breath, and it made a raspberry sound; then he muttered, "Oh, man" under his breath. "Alright," he said a little louder. He plopped down on the dock, dripping water everywhere while he dangled his long, toned legs in the crystal-clear lake.

I sat beside him and waited impatiently for him to speak.

He sighed heavily yet again before he finally opened his mouth. "I told you a bit about my childhood…growing up and being teased all the time…"

I nodded.

"Well…when I turned fifteen, everything changed for me. The kids that once ridiculed me and pushed me around suddenly wanted to be my friend. I should have put the connection together right away, but I was so young, and I just wanted to be accepted so damn bad." He sighed again. "I never told anyone that my family had money. It wasn't something that I ever bragged about...but, well...one day, one of my friends, Brock, took a stand on my behalf. He started spreading rumors that I had my own yacht somewhere with a beach house...and that I owned a cabin on the lake..." He paused and laughed softly. "Even though only a few of his exaggerations were true, people started taking notice. I finally understood the saying 'money talks'. And soon, I became everyone's best friend. All the guys who had picked on me the day before were wanting to come hang out at my house and watch movies in our home theater. The girls who had been whispering and giggling behind my back suddenly became interested in me, giving me compliments and hanging on my every word. They would beg to come over and go swimming...which is where the issues with Cora came in. Some of the girls that would show up to the parties would sneak upstairs and go through Cora's stuff; sometimes they'd even take some of her clothes and her jewelry. But my adolescent thought process was, 'Why should I care, right? I mean, we have money, we can just replace materialistic things.' I didn't realize that all those stupid kids were just using me...or maybe I just didn't really care, because I was finally being treated like everybody else. No one was judging me for my looks...so I wasn't considered different anymore. But as the years went on, the parties got bigger, and so did the problems. I started feeling like I was this hotshot who had everything and everyone at his fingertips. I felt untouchable...invincible even. I eventually became reckless and out of control, drinking...experimenting with drugs...sleeping around..." Alec blew out his breath and looked out toward the lake. "I'm not proud of some of the things I've done...and it's hard to talk about all this...especially with you."

I began to feel slightly offended. "Why, 'especially with

me?'"

Alec still would not look my way. "Because I didn't have my financial safety net when it came to you. You were the first girl to care about me…for me. And that scared the living daylights out of me. Still does. Things were great from behind the computer screen; I could just be myself. I didn't have to show off. I didn't have to go out of my way to impress you. Things were simple. But then you asked to meet, and I didn't know what to do; so that's why I constantly acted like a childish asshole." His gaze slowly shifted to mine. "I knew what we had was a genuine connection right from the start…it was real…there were no strings attached…there was nothing forcing you to be in my life. So, I was always worried that I could lose you…which I know now how stupid my way of thinking was, but that's all I'd ever known, so…"

I sat there, slightly stunned, finally understanding the shift in his demeanor when things got serious between us, and why Cora was so pissed-off when she saw me in one of her suits. In her mind, I must have been just another selfish little wannabe that was trying to take advantage of her brother…and her family's money. Those realizations made me both sad and angry.

"So, that's pretty much everything," he finished.

I sat there quietly for quite some time, moving my feet back and forth in the water, letting everything sink in.

Alec sighed again. "I've messed this up, haven't I?"

I glanced in his direction, seeing that his head was angled down, his brow was furrowed, and his fists were clenched against the dock, holding onto the edge so tight that the wood audibly creaked in protest.

The confusion and frustration that had filled me only a few seconds ago seemed to melt away. A sad smile tugged at my lips as I gently bumped my shoulder against his. "Everyone has a past, Alec," I replied quietly.

His head instantly turned toward me. The distressed

expression on his face didn't change, but his hands slowly relaxed.

I sighed once more. "I can't say that I'm happy to hear about all those things...the drinking, the drugs, the girls...but I'm not with you for whoever you used to be; I'm with you for the man you are now."

He smiled then. "You have no idea how relieved I am to hear that."

"You should know better." That time, I gave his shoulder a hard shove, and he feigned losing his balance before falling into the water, splashing me from head to toe. The look on his face when he resurfaced made me laugh.

"Will you join me now?" he asked sweetly.

I didn't verbally reply. Instead, I eased myself off the dock and into his awaiting arms.

Alec smiled while biting his bottom lip as he ran his fingers through my hair. "You really don't think differently about me after hearing things from my past?"

I shook my head and leaned into his touch. "Not even a little bit."

~*~*~*~

Alec and I ended up staying for dinner...mostly because his parents insisted. They refused to let us leave without having full bellies.

We laughed and traded stories from our past while joking around and getting to know each other better. Alec actually blushed a few times when his mother talked about his childhood. It was the most adorable thing I had ever seen. The only downside was that Cora didn't say a single word to me the whole night...or to Alec for that matter...but I tried not to let that bother me.

After we had eaten, Lindy excused herself and disappeared into the next room.

Alec was sitting with one elbow on the table, leaning his cheek against his fist as the plates were being cleared away. Then suddenly he glanced up. "Oh, c'mon, mom! Don't bring out the old photo albums...ohh, no...aaaand here we go!" He covered his face and chuckled.

Lindy smiled while ignoring her son's pleas as she dragged her chair closer to mine and placed two large albums on the table in front of me. "I've never had the pleasure of embarrassing my sweet boy in front of his girlfriend, so this is quite exciting."

"Look away, Scarlett! Look away!" Alec said jokingly as he stretched his long arms across the table and tried to grab the closest photo album.

Lindy swatted at him playfully. "You'd better leave those alone, young man! Let me brag about my handsome son for a little while!"

"Yeah, Alec," Cora finally spoke up. "It's not like you've ever had a decent girl to bring home before. So, this is a new experience for everyone."

"Cora!" Lindy said sternly. "You will not be disrespectful to guests in this house!"

I sat there quietly with my eyes angled down towards the table.

The tension in the room at that point could have been cut with a knife; but after a few minutes, Alec forced a laugh to ease the discomfort. "It's okay, mom...big sister is right. This is a new experience."

Cora shrugged while staring at her brother. "Hey, I'm not the one hiding behind a façade, trying to impress anybody." With that, she stood, scraping her chair lightly against the marble floor. "I've gotta head out. Thanks for dinner, mom. I'll see you tomorrow." Then she kissed her mother on the cheek.

Lindy caught her daughter's wrist and gently pulled her down to whisper something in her ear.

The two of them stared at each other for a second or two before Cora sighed and gave her mother a hug. "Okay, yeah. I will. I love you."

"I love you, too, sweetie. Be sure to say goodbye to your

dad before you go."

"I will," she replied reassuringly. Then she looked directly at me.

I swallowed nervously under her scrutinizing gaze.

Alec suddenly jumped up and walked over to his sister. He lowered his voice so that neither Lindy nor I could hear him.

Cora stared at her brother for a few seconds with a slightly perplexed expression. "Are you serious?"

Alec nodded. "Most definitely."

Cora sighed. "Well, then don't screw it up. And for the love of God, keep Brock away."

Alec smirked and held out his closed fist. "Deal."

Cora's hardened shell seemed to soften a bit as she glanced up at him with a questioning stare.

Alec's smile widened.

Cora chuckled half-heartedly as she held up her fist and bonked it gently against his. Then they both made the sound of a miniature explosion before giving each other a high five.

Lindy let out a soft laugh. "Well, that's something I haven't seen for many years. Your secret handshake." Then she turned to me. "They would always wait until they thought their father and I weren't looking. As if we didn't know what they were up to."

A quiet laugh escaped my lips. "That's too cute."

"Of course it's cute!" Alec blurted out. "I made it up!"

"Ohh, you are so full of shit!" Cora retorted. "I'm the one that came up with the little explosion part with the high five at the end."

"Psht!" Alec waved her words away. "You wish you were that clever."

The three Cavanaughs laughed.

Alec hugged his sister as tight as he could. "See ya, my sistah from anothah mistah!"

Cora rolled her eyes and snort-laughed while still in his arms. "You are such a dork." She let go and gave his shoulder a gentle punch. "I'll see you later, little bro." Then she abruptly turned towards me. "It was honestly nice to meet you, Scarlett. And I'm sorry if I said anything that may have upset you. I know now that I had the wrong impression."

I cleared my throat and shifted slightly in my seat. Her words had completely taken me by surprise. "It's alright." I cleared my throat again. "It was nice to meet you, too."

A short while later, after Cora had said goodbye to her father and gone home, Alec and Lindy resumed their playful arguing.

Lindy opened one of the photo albums and turned it to the first page. "If you don't want to reminisce with your dear old mother, Alec, then by all means, take yourself into the living room with your dad. Scarlett and I are perfectly capable of enjoying ourselves without you."

Alec chuckled. "I think I'll stick around to keep an eye on you two...especially my dear old mother."

"Old?" Lindy repeated. She narrowed her eyes and scoffed. Then much to my surprise, that elegant woman, in her beautifully tailored dress, decked out with diamonds and pearls, looked right at her son and actually stuck her tongue out as a response.

Alec's laughter echoed throughout the house. "I was only reiterating exactly what you just said!"

I was grinning from ear to ear while listening to them go back and forth. It was beyond precious to watch him interact with his family, especially his mother. The love they had for each other made my heart swell.

Lindy's face softened as she smirked. "Never agree with a woman when they say they are old, fat, or ugly. It is always the opposite. Understood?"

Alec did a little salute. "Yes, ma'am. Understood."

Lindy smiled wider. "Good! Now back to bragging about my precious little boy!"

"Oh, God...why me?" Alec muttered quietly while

looking up toward the ceiling. The smirk on his face caused me to nearly choke on my water.

Lindy patted my back while speaking to her son. "When you have children of your own someday, you will finally understand how this feels."

Alec's playful demeanor instantly disappeared. "Mom, we've talked about this." His tone was dead serious.

She waved her hand at him. "You can adopt. We've talked about that, too."

Alec's gaze instantly shifted toward me, then back to his mother. "Can we not discuss this right now? It's a bit inappropriate, don't you think?"

"Why?" Lindy inquired. "Does Scarlett not want children?" She turned to me. "Do you not want children, dear?"

"MOM!" Alec's voice reverberated throughout the room. "This isn't something that Scarlett and I have..." He paused and sighed. "We've only just met in person. That's not the type of thing you just bring up out of nowhere."

"It's a perfectly natural thing for couples to talk about, Alec. Why, your dad and I discussed how many children we wanted while we were on our very first date!" She smiled at the memory.

Alec sighed again. "That's you and dad...it's not..."

"I do want to have kids," I interrupted while giving him a what-the-hell-is-wrong-with-you stare. "Someday." I smiled at his mom and shrugged. "I think it would be amazing to have a child with the man I love. To see a part of each of us in their little face..."

Alec suddenly stood up so forcefully that his chair toppled backward. Then he stormed out of the room.

I started to stand to go after him, but Lindy placed her hand on my shoulder and sighed. "Let me talk to him, dear. I'm afraid that I may have crossed a line that he..."

"It was an innocent question," I told her. "Something that would have been discussed between us at some point."

Lindy smiled faintly. "I'm sure it would have been, but..." She sighed again. "I shouldn't have put my nose in his business, especially when it comes to this." She patted my shoulder again. "I won't be long. Hopefully he will forgive his meddlesome mother."

I offered her a brief smile before she walked away. I listened to the sound of her soft footfalls heading upstairs. I thought about joining Alec's father in the next room, but I didn't want to interrupt whatever he was doing.

After about ten minutes had passed, I decided to open one of the photo albums. As I began flipping through it, Alec's adorable face greeted me again and again. The first few pages were from when he was just a few months old. Then it shifted into his toddler years, where a different story was told. He was in the hospital in some of them, recovering from some sort of procedure or surgery. Same for his grade-school years. I closed the album and set it on top of the other one just as Lindy and Alec reappeared side by side in the archway.

"Is everything okay?" I asked hesitantly.

Lindy smiled briefly. "Of course! Nothing that a mother's love couldn't fix."

Alec chuckled. "I love you, too, mom." He turned his attention to me. "Are you ready to go?"

I raised an eyebrow. "Already?"

He nodded. "It's nearly midnight. And we've still got a bit of driving to do."

I stared at him skeptically. "Seriously?" Then I glanced up at the clock. "Oh, my goodness," I laughed. "It is!"

"The photos and bragging will have to wait until your next visit," Lindy announced. Her tone was a mixture of sadness and amusement.

"Dodged a bullet," Alec muttered under his breath.

Lindy smacked his arm in a less-than-gentle manner. "Hush you!"

Alec laughed and rubbed his bicep as if it hurt. "Would

this be classified as child abuse?"

All three of us were laughing then.

"The only time you or your sister ever got your butts popped was if you deserved it! And I never hit you too hard!"

Alec hugged his mother. "I know, mom. I'm just teasing you."

Lindy tugged me closer as she hugged both of us at the same time. "I have had such a wonderful time today!" She squeezed her son, "You need to come by more often! I miss you and your sister so much since you both moved out." Then she squeezed me, "And you, my dear, need to come over more often as well! You are officially part of the family now! So, no need to call beforehand. You just show up anytime! With or without my handsome son."

Alec and I both chuckled. "We will," we both said in unison.

After saying goodbye to Henry, and one last group hug, Alec and I headed outside.

CHAPTER 16

Alec was quiet for the entire drive back to his apartment. I wasn't sure if he had something specific on his mind, or if he was just tired after such a long day. But when we pulled into the parking lot for the apartment complex, the silence that had been consuming us completely disappeared.

"What the hell…?" Alec blurted out.

I followed his gaze.

Three police cars, all flashing their lights, were parked in front of Alec's building…directly behind my car. A small crowd was gathering; all huddled together on Alec's neighbor's front lawn.

"What do you think is going on?" I asked as I leaned forward, surveying the surrounding area.

"I'm not sure," Alec replied as he slowed to a crawl and approached the closest police car. He rolled down his window and propped his elbow up on the sill. "Evening, officer. May I ask what's going on?"

"Possible missing person's case. Do you live around here?"

"This is my apartment," Alec replied, gesturing toward

his front door.

The officer immediately reached for his radio, but before he had a chance to say a word, a girl resembling Liza abruptly appeared behind him, make-up smeared and tears streaming down her face.

Alec turned toward me. "Um, I think we may be in a bit of trouble."

I looked at him confused. "Huh? Why?"

He gestured behind the group of officers hovering around my car. Sure enough, my best friend was standing in front of them, frantically pointing and shouting, all while crying hysterically.

"Oh, my God!" I cried out. I opened the passenger door and jumped out. "LIZA!" I screamed. "LIZA, WHAT HAPPENED?"

My best friend's head instantly snapped up and her eyes immediately locked onto mine. "SCARLETT?" she shouted frantically. "OH, MY GOSH! SCARLETT!" A split second later, she began running towards me.

We collided in the middle of the parking lot, latching onto one another.

"What happened?" I asked her. "What's wrong?"

Liza was nearly choking on her own words when she replied, "I thought...something had happened to you! I hadn't heard from you...since last night...when you chased after Alec...so I...I called the police this morning! I thought you were missing...or worse!" She clutched me closer as sobs continued to rack her body. "I practically turned your room upside down looking for the box with his address on it...then I came here as fast as I could."

I squeezed her tight, realizing what a horribly selfish person I had been. I hadn't even given her, or anyone else, a second thought while I was with Alec. "I am so sorry, Liza! I should have called you...I should have let you know what was going on! I'm sorry! I just got so caught up in the moment. I promise that I will never let this happen again!"

While I was profusely apologizing, Alec parked his car in a random parking space and eventually made his way over to us. "Is everything alright?" he asked quietly.

Liza pulled away from my embrace, tears still pouring from her puffy eyes. "No!" she snapped. "Everything is most definitely *not* alright! Where have you been? Where did you take her? What have you been doing to her?"

Alec's hands went up in a defensive position as his eyes widened and he took a couple steps back. "Whoa, calm down, Liza. Scarlett is fine. We were just visiting my family."

Liza was beyond distraught by that point, which caused a few of the police officers to approach with caution. One pulled Alec to the side, with his hand on his holster. That made me extremely nervous. A split second later, another officer asked to speak with me privately, leading me in the opposite direction.

"Miss Mitchel? Can you please tell me your whereabouts over the last twenty-four hours?"

From where I was standing, I could see Alec in my peripheral vision. He had his hands on his hips, and he was shaking his head. Occasionally, he would point at me or gesture toward his front door.

After answering a few questions, and proving that I wasn't being held prisoner, the series of events finally seemed to add up enough for the officers to get a clear picture; and to see that the situation was just a misunderstanding from a lack of communication…mostly on my part.

Both Alec's and my responses had been nearly identical, so after the officers were able to calm Liza down, they left.

There was no way that I could let my best friend go home at nearly two o'clock in the morning when she was that upset, so I asked Alec if she could stay in his guest room. His response was exactly what I knew it would be, "Of course."

The instant Liza's head hit the pillow, she was out. I guess the stress and anxiety of the last twenty-four hours had really gotten to her...which made me feel absolutely horrible. I kissed her cheek and whispered, "I'm sorry" a few more times before shutting the door and joining Alec in his living room.

I plopped down on the couch beside him. "Crazy day, huh?"

He sighed. "Yeah. Pretty crazy." That look of intensity was back on his face again.

"What cha thinkin' about?"

Another sigh escaped his lips. "Nothing really."

I scoffed and smiled. "That's clearly a lie. You've got your thinking-face on."

He turned and grinned at me. "My thinking-face, eh?"

"Mm-hmm. It looks like this..." I strained my facial muscles, furrowing my brow, and pursing my lips in an attempt to mimic his features.

Alec laughed. "Mm-hmm. That looks exactly like me."

I rolled my eyes playfully. "Are you just gonna keep repeating everything I say tonight, or are you gonna tell me what's on your mind?"

"I think I'm just gonna keep repeating everything you say tonight..."

I placed my hand over his mouth as he continued to mumble the rest of the words.

Then we both started laughing.

I cleared my throat to stop my giggles. "C'mon, Alec. Be serious for a second."

"I'm sorry," he chuckled. "I'm trying." Then his smile slowly faded away. "I just..." He sighed. "I can't stop thinking about what my mom said after dinner. Normally, I don't get angry when she brings it up...but tonight...with you there...it just got under my skin...and now I can't seem to get it out of my head."

"Is it because you don't want kids, and I said that I do?"

He shook his head. "No. I *do* want kids…eventually, but it's a bit more complicated for someone like me."

"Are you unsure if you can have them?"

His entire body tensed.

"I'm sorry," I said quickly. "I didn't mean to get overly personal about this."

He sighed again and turned toward me, caressing my face while moving a strand of hair behind my ear. "It's not that. I'm open to discussing anything with you. It's just…" He sighed once again as his hand lingered against my cheek. "I've never had this type of conversation with anyone outside of my immediate family, so it's a bit…unnerving."

I leaned into his touch. "Well, then we don't have to talk about it right now if you don't want to."

"No," he whispered. "You should know about this. Especially if we ever decide to take things further in our relationship…ya know…with marriage, and possibly starting a family…"

I smiled at his words.

Alec blew out his breath as his hands fell away from my face. "…but, I'm afraid it's not that simple."

"Why not?" I frowned.

His perfect smile slowly returned. "Well, to answer your question, as far as I know, my 'baby maker' is in perfect working order…"

A grin tugged at my lips. "So, then what is the problem?"

Alec's happy demeanor was soon mixed with sadness. "It has to do with my syndrome."

I stared at him while his eyes grew distant.

"Someone with the gene for Treacher Collins can pass it on to their children," he continued. "There's a fifty-fifty chance that any child I have will be born with it. So, needless to say, it's something I've been going back and forth with for years."

"But even with those odds, there's still a chance that you could have a child without it."

"That small of a chance isn't worth it to me. I just don't think I could handle knowing that I was the cause of any struggles my future son or daughter would have to endure. All the painful surgeries to help with their hearing or breathing, and then the slow agonizing recoveries afterward. Not to mention, the constant stares and ridicule from uneducated strangers." He paused and sighed once again as his eyes started to glisten. "I struggled for years to love and accept myself. And honestly, it would kill me to see my child in any kind of pain...physical or emotional...because I was selfish for a chance to have a little human being with my DNA."

"I can understand that."

Alec sighed deeply. "I know it may be asking a lot from my future wife...to give up the chance to have a biological child..."

"There is always the option of using a donor," I interrupted him. "...or even adoption if that doesn't work out."

Alec raked his hands through his hair and leaned his elbows on his knees to where I could no longer see his face. "Yeah, I know. My mom said the same thing, but I just..." He paused to take in a deep breath, letting it out slowly. "It's a very sensitive subject for me...for a lot of personal reasons. But honestly," he paused again, "I'm just too tired to have this type of emotional conversation right now. I'd rather go to bed and discuss it tomorrow after we've both had some sleep...if that's okay?"

I placed my hand on his back reassuringly. "Of course. I'm actually ready for bed myself. Do you mind if I borrow some of your clothes again so I can take a shower?"

Alec instantly looked my way. His dark hair falling across most of his face, but it didn't hide his smirk. "I think that can be arranged."

A second or so later, he stood and offered me his hand.

~*~*~*~

By the time I had taken my shower and brushed my teeth, Alec was already curled up beneath his navy-blue duvet.

"Are you asleep?" I whispered as I tiptoed closer.

Alec stirred, raising his head to look in my direction. "Nope. I'm wide awake," he yawned.

I chuckled lightly as I climbed into his bed and slipped under the covers beside him.

Without any prompting, Alec shifted closer, pulling me against his body and wrapping his arms around me. After a few seconds of silence, he whispered, "I'd want to go with adoption over a donor." His warm exhale tingled against the back of my neck.

My eyes closed on their own accord. "You still don't want to tell me why?"

His body shifted away from me ever so slightly. "It sounds too selfish to say out loud."

By his words and his actions, I could tell how badly Alec yearned to have a child of his own, but his desire to spare them from experiencing the burden of unnecessary struggles outweighed everything else.

I abruptly turned over so I could face him. Almost immediately, he propped himself up. His bright blue eyes shone through the darkness like vibrant sparkling pools, staring into the depths of my soul.

"Whatever you want…is what I want," I whispered.

He studied my face for what seemed like an eternity…then he smiled. "You are truly amazing, ya know that?"

"So are you," I replied quietly.

Alec's perfect smile widened as he pulled me back into his arms, leaning his head against mine. "Goodnight, my dearest Scarlett," he said groggily.

I sighed blissfully as I snuggled closer to him. "Goodnight, Alec."

<u>CHAPTER 17</u>

I woke up to the sound of a door slamming and then someone shouting Alec's name.

"You missed out on one hell of a night, my man," a male voice called out.

I reflexively reached out beside me, expecting to feel Alec's warm body, but the sheets were cold. A tell-tale sign that he had been up for quite some time.

Then I heard Alec reply from the other end of the apartment, "I'm sure I didn't miss that much."

The other man chuckled. "There were so many women throwing themselves at me; you would have had the time of your life! And before I forget, Vanessa and Sabrina were asking about you. You shoulda seen the looks on their faces when I told them that you were out with some chick you had met online. They were pissed-off to hell that you blew them off again. But anyway, how did it go? Did you hit that or what?"

"Dude, keep your voice down!" Alec snapped.

"Ohhhh, shit! Is she here?" the other man asked.

"She's sleeping."

The man lowered his voice, "So it was good?"

"Brock. Shut up!"

My heart instantly crumbled and my stomach tightened. I jumped out of Alec's bed and slipped into his line of sight.

The man who he had been talking to turned and grinned at me while looking me up and down. "Niiiiiice," he said while nodding his head approvingly. Then he held his hand up in the air as if waiting for Alec to give him a high five.

I could feel my face turning beet red, mostly from embarrassment, but partially from anger. Alec didn't even say anything on my behalf, which nearly broke my heart.

Tears stung my eyes as I ran to the bathroom and locked the door behind me. *How could I have been so stupid? So naïve? Of course, he turns out to be a player! That's just my luck! So much for his past being kept in the past.*

Not even a second later, the knob jiggled, and Alec knocked on the bathroom door. "Scarlett? Scarlett, open the door, please. Let me explain. It's not what you think."

"Go away, Alec!" I replied. I wanted my voice to sound strong, but it didn't at all.

I heard his cocky friend say something, but I couldn't make out what it was.

"Shut up, Brock!" Alec called out. Then his attention was back on me. "Scarlett, please…open the door, sweetheart."

"Sweetheart my ass!" I took one last look in the mirror while ignoring his pleas, then I inhaled a deep breath and prepared to make my exit. I turned the lock and flung the door open as hard as I could, only half caring that I actually smacked Alec right in the face.

I shoved past him and headed back to his room, where I began gathering up all my clothes that were currently strewn all over the floor. A few happened to be near the opened closet door, which was when my eyes landed on the box of Alec's sister's clothes. It hadn't stuck out to me until then, that many of them were different sizes. I paused and let out a small sigh. "These aren't just Cora's things...are they?"

After a brief pause, Alec sighed. "Scarlett..." And that was all he got out. Just my name as a response.

"I guess that's my answer," I whispered. The cold, hard truth of reality finally slapped me right in the face. The entire box was filled with items that had been left behind from other girls who had probably stayed the night with him over the years. *How perfect.*

"Would you have let me prance around in some other random girl's clothes without...?" I couldn't even finish my sentence.

Against my will, I began to imagine Alec carrying countless faceless women down the hall and into his room. I imagined him laying them down onto his bed...caressing their faces...touching their bodies...whispering the same sweet nothings into their ear...before making love to them exactly the same way he had made love to me.

More tears pricked my eyes as images of the last couple days came flooding back.

The whole time that I was picking up my belongings, Alec was standing in his doorway watching me.

I stood up straight, clutching everything in my arms, unable to take the silence anymore. "It was all bullshit, wasn't it?" I cried out. "The sorry-ass sob story you fed me? Pretending to be this vulnerable, self-conscious, sweet-talking gentleman...when in reality, you're still just the same playboy...seeking attention and acceptance any way you can get it! And to top it all off, you had the audacity to take me to meet your family...acting like I was someone special! How many women are there in your life right now, Alec? Was I just some piece-of-ass to you...like all those girls from your past? A conquest? That's nice to know after everything we've been through!"

He stared at me with his mouth hanging open and his eyes wide. "Are you kidding me? No! Hell no! That's not what this is! Scarlett, you know me...you know that's not..."

When he reached out for me, I jerked my arm away. "Get your filthy hands off me!" I shrieked.

He took a few steps back and swallowed. His face was covered in what I would have described as shame and regret, but I chalked that up to him getting caught in his lies.

I stormed past him, and then past his stupid-ass friend, who would not even meet my gaze anymore.

I banged on the guest bedroom door as hard as I could. "Liza! Liza, we need to go!" When there was no response, I opened the door.

She was lying on the bed with her Walkman resting in her lap, headphones in her ears. When she noticed my tear-stained cheeks, she immediately yanked the headphones off and got up. "What's wrong?"

"We're leaving," I said sternly.

She didn't even bother to ask for a more in-depth reason. Instead, my best friend followed me out of the room.

I grabbed my keys off the counter and then Liza and I rushed straight outside. I flung my stuff into the back seat of my car while Liza headed for the passenger side.

"What about your car?" I asked her.

"I'll ask Derek to bring me by later to pick it up. Let's just go."

By the time I had climbed into the driver's seat, Alec was halfway down the stairs.

He didn't even bother using the last few steps as he hopped down onto the sidewalk and stood beside my door. One of his hands was on the roof; the other was holding onto the handle to keep the door ajar. "Don't go, babe," he pleaded. "Please. Brock is an asshole, and he blurts out a lot of idiotic and inappropriate shit, but you just have to take what he says with a grain of salt…or just ignore him like I do."

"You stood there and let him talk about me like I was nothing! Why don't you go call *Vanessa* and *Sabrina* since they are probably soooo concerned about you right now!" I said their names with so much hatred, but I could not seem to help it.

I gently shoved him back to get him out of the way so I could shut the driver's side door, which I ended up slamming a bit too hard.

Liza hit the automatic door locks.

I revved the engine a few times while I started to back up, but then Alec got the brilliant idea to position himself directly in my path. "Son of a...," I grumbled under my breath. I dialed down the rage brewing inside me and slowed to a crawl, so I didn't run his lying ass over.

Slowly and carefully I continued to back up, forcing him to retreat without physical injury. His hands were on the trunk of my car while he continued to walk backwards, still begging me not to go, insisting that it was just another misunderstanding.

When I saw him step up on the curb, I quickly shifted into drive and peeled out of the parking lot before he had any time to get in front of my car to block me again.

When I was finally driving down the interstate, I let the tears fall, blurring my vision as we headed back home.

"What the hell happened?" Liza finally asked. "I thought everything was like a fairytale with you guys."

"So did I. But it turns out that I wasn't the only one that he..." I just couldn't get the words out.

I could see Liza's expression shift from concern to sorrow. "Oh, bestie. I am so sorry."

I didn't want to talk about it anymore. My vision was already coming and going, and I didn't want to wreck the car. So, I turned up the radio and tried to drown out my thoughts.

CHAPTER 18

When Liza and I finally turned onto our street, a glint of silver caught my eye in the rearview mirror.

As I slowed to a stop in front of our condo, Alec parked his Camaro directly behind my car, letting his engine idle. He must have been flying to catch up to us so fast.

"He seriously followed us home?" Liza scoffed. "Unbelievable!"

"I can't face him right now," I whimpered.

"You don't have to," my best friend stated confidently. "Just wait here. I'll take care of it."

Before I had a chance to even remove my keys from the ignition, Liza had hopped out of the car and was walking towards our unwanted guest.

I opened my door and called out her name just in time to see her slap Alec right across the face.

I covered my mouth by reflex as I watched him stumble backward; thankfully he caught himself on the hood of his car, so he didn't hit the pavement.

"That was just a warning shot, buddy!" Liza threatened. Then she held up both fists while staring him down. "If you ever come near my best friend again, I will tear your ass apart! DO YOU HEAR ME?!"

The stunned expression remained on his face while he regained his footing; then he started trying to explain himself, to which Liza swung at him again, but he dodged it.

I couldn't stand the sight of him anymore, so I ran toward the front door, listening to Liza screaming at Alec, and Alec screaming for me.

~*~*~*~

The house phone didn't stop ringing for the rest of the afternoon...and well into the evening. In fact, the phone didn't stop ringing for days on end.

The answering machine was repeatedly filled with Alec's messages.

"Scarlett, please call me."

"Scarlett, if you'd just let me explain..."

"Please answer my calls...or at least respond to my emails!"

"Dammit, Scarlett...I know you're there! Please pick up!"

"That's it; I'm coming to your house!"

And he did.

Every. Single. Day. For weeks.

Even after Liza's threats, he refused to give up.

You name it, Alec used it to try to get in touch with me. Emails. AOL Instant Messenger. Calls. Even that idiot, Brock, called on his best friend's behalf. But I never gave in. I couldn't. I just couldn't. Not after what I had heard. He had used me. He had played me like a fool. And there was no coming back from that. Ever.

One particular day, things seemed to be spiraling for me, and I just couldn't handle it anymore. Hearing his voice hurt my heart so much, and he just would not stop calling.

The messages on the answering machine that afternoon consisted of him begging for me to talk to him. Of course, he was crying. So, needless to say, I had to delete it before hearing the entire thing.

The next three messages consisted of songs. The first one was 'Always' by Jon Bon Jovi; the second was 'Hard To Say I'm Sorry' by Chicago; and the third was 'Against All Odds' by Phil Collins. I was sobbing uncontrollably by that point. And the red light was still blinking, but I just could not listen to anymore.

It was like an endless loop of verbal torment, constantly entering my ears and forcing me to relive the past against my will.

Liza eventually disconnected the phone jack from the wall, but that only pushed Alec to come by in person on a daily basis. Which was even worse.

He would show up at random times throughout the day, even in the middle of the night, throwing pebbles at my window to try and get my attention.

A few times, he even slept on the stairs of our little front porch. I will never forget opening the door and having him literally fall inside the house. The startled scream that came out of my mouth probably woke up the entire neighborhood.

Liza quickly escorted him back to his car...not that it helped matters much. He made an appearance at my job that same afternoon, but thankfully, my wonderful boss and co-workers put a stop to that real quick.

Still, the messages never ceased. The flowers and cards full of apologies never stopped being delivered. And the emails continued to filter in. I had reached my breaking point and desperately needed to get away. Far, far away.

I wheeled my suitcase into the living room just as Liza was finishing up with a call. I could hear her yelling...words that I would not dare repeat. My mouth is not that foul.

"If you call back again, Alec, I will have a restraining order taken out on you! Do you hear me? Scarlett's dad is a cop, remember?" Liza paused and laughed forcefully. "Try it, dude! See how serious I am! Just leave her the hell alone! The damage is done, and she's moved on! You need to do the same!" Liza growled as she slammed the phone down on the receiver.

"I think I've got everything packed that I'll need," I announced.

She whirled around and sighed. "I can't believe he's making you flee from your own home. It's like he's turned into some crazy creeper who has ruined your life!"

"A crazy creeper living in his grandmother's basement?"

Liza grinned. "Who collects his own belly button lint."

We both laughed. Something we had not done in a while.

Liza walked me out to my car. She hugged me so tight that all the air was squeezed from my lungs. "You just take care of you, okay? Don't give this ridiculous situation another thought."

I sighed. "I'll try."

~*~*~*~

A few days later, I was sitting on the front porch swing at my parent's two-story log cabin, drinking a warm cup of cocoa, listening to the soothing sounds of the water rushing through a nearby creek. The wind gently rustled the trees, sending leaves and little branches floating to the ground.

Late autumn in the countryside was extremely beautiful…and just what I needed. I had not thought about Alec at all since I had arrived. Not even once.

Okay, so that was clearly a lie.

The truth was, I could *not* stop thinking about him. The guy had me feeling like a stupid teenage girl with a stupid teenage crush. And those feelings got even stronger after I came across a letter he had written to me.

In my rush to leave Alec's apartment that fateful day, I didn't realize that I had grabbed Cora's ripped-up jeans by mistake. So, when Liza was helping me pack for my trip, she must have tossed them into my suitcase, thinking they were mine. What I found in one of the pockets caused me to burst into tears…

My dearest Scarlett,

You are sound asleep in my bed right now, looking like an angel.

I want to tell you how much my heart aches for you...and how much my body craves to feel the touch of your skin...the embrace of your loving arms...and the intensity within your gentle grasp.

My hands need to know what it's like to feel our fingers entwined. I yearn for the sweet caress of your lips as they brush against mine, even if only for a moment. My mind swirls with thoughts of you, wondering what each precious moment would be like when we finally become one.

I know I don't show it as often as I should, but you are the most precious thing in my life. When I look at you, it's as if time stands still, and we are the only two people in the universe.

My tears cannot decide if they should fall for happiness, fear, or sadness.

Happiness because I've found you...

Fear that you'll stop caring about me, or leave me...

And sadness because I may not be able to have you the way that I want to.

Anything you ever ask for, my reply will always be: As you wish.

Yours always, Alec

Too bad those heart-stopping words turned out to be part of his little game.

"Scarlett, honey," my mom abruptly called out, derailing my thoughts. "Liza is on the phone."

"Coming!" I stopped the swing from moving and headed inside. I smiled as I took the receiver from my mom's hand. "Hey, chickadee. What's up?"

"Oh, ya know, the usual," Liza replied. "So..."

My eyebrow raised. "Soooo...what?"

She literally growled at me. "Don't make me beg for details," she blurted out. "Look, I'm sorry that I told him where you were. I know that makes me like *the* worst best friend in the world, but Scarlett, he was crying! I mean, he was so distraught, literally choking on his own sobs into the phone. He explained everything...down to the smallest detail...and I actually listened. Call me a wimp, a puss, whatever...but I'm woman enough to admit it...I caved. I gave him your parents' number...and the address, too. But he said he wouldn't call because he didn't want you to disappear before he could get there to..."

"Liza..." I interrupted, "...you told Alec how to get here?"

She sighed. "Yeah...wait... Is he not...? Did he not...?"

"He's not here," I informed her.

"That's impossible," she stated. "He left yesterday afternoon. He would have been there last night at the latest."

"He's not here," I said again. My mind was spinning. "Maybe he stopped at a hotel to gather some courage or something."

"Let me call you back," Liza told me.

The line disconnected before I had time to say anything else. I placed the receiver back on its base and waited. Not even a minute later, the line rang again.

"Hey..." I answered halfway through the first ring. "So, what's going on?"

Liza sighed and then it was silent for a second or two. "Scarlett...Brock is at Alec's place taking care of Sarge. He said that Alec left around two-thirty yesterday afternoon. So, even if he made a few stops along the way, he should have gotten to your parent's house sometime in the evening."

My heart instantly dropped. Then it was my turn to say, "I'll call you back."

"Okay," Liza breathed.

I hung up and rushed to the kitchen. "Dad?" I called out. "Can we take your cruiser down the mountain towards town?"

"Uh, sure, sweetie," his voice returned. "Why? Is something wrong with your car?"

I grabbed his keys from the hook in the hall and waited for him by the front door. "I'm hoping I'm wrong, but I think Alec was coming to see me…and he should have been here last night…"

The temperature the night before had dropped into the low thirties, near freezing.

As if my reply was all he needed, my dad said, "Let's go," and he quickly ushered me out the door.

CHAPTER 19

As we drove down the mountainside, easing through all the twists and turns of the winding roads, we both scanned each side for any signs of a disturbance. We slowed to a crawl as we approached Reaper's Ditch, which was rightly named for all the accidents that happened on the sharp ninety-degree curve.

Halfway through the bend, my heart tightened in my chest. "Daddy! STOP!" I cried out.

I already had the passenger door open before the words were even out of my mouth. My dad slammed on the breaks, causing the car to jerk to an abrupt halt just as I stumbled out onto the street.

"Scarlett!" he called after me. "Be careful!"

I heard him radioing dispatch for help while I ran as fast as I could, jumping over what was left of the recently damaged metal guardrail.

I skid and slid down the mountain slope, following the path of destruction, all while screaming Alec's name at the top of my lungs.

I saw a faint stream of smoke before I saw the actual

vehicle, but deep down in the core of my soul I already knew whose car it was going to be.

The ground was wet, thanks to a late afternoon thunderstorm, causing the tread on my shoes to slip on the patches of moss covering the soggy ground. The thick underbrush also slowed down my progress as I tripped over small trees that had been knocked down and snapped in half during Alec's accelerated descent.

Oh God, no!

His silver Camaro finally came into view...well, the top half of it anyway. The vehicle was on its side, wedged between two young pine trees and a ginormous boulder.

"ALEC!" I screamed. "ALEC, I'M COMING!"

The closer I got to the wreckage, the more damage I was able to see. All of the windows, including the front and back windshields, had been busted out. And thick shards of glass were everywhere.

For a split second, I wondered if he had even survived the crash, but I pushed that morbid thought out of my head.

I made my way around to the back of the car, then attempted to use the rough edges of the boulder to pull myself up. I immediately noticed that the front left tire was missing, and the right tire was bent at such a strange angle that the entire wheel was flat against the underside of the car.

Older vehicles were much stronger than any new piece of fiberglass driving down the road. So, for that type of damage, Alec had to have been going at a very high speed around that curve.

I finally managed to scramble up onto the oversized rock. I leaned over and peered inside. When Alec's limp and seemingly lifeless body came into view, a quiet whimper escaped my lips, causing his head to slowly shift in my direction.

"Help...me," he said hoarsely, his teeth chattering.

I choked back a sob as my gaze landed on a deep laceration on the right side of his forehead. Part of his skull was exposed through the gash, which caused my stomach to do an uneasy flip. The trails of blood running down his cheeks were dry and crusted, which made me wonder exactly how long he had been trapped like that.

"Scarlett?" he asked quietly.

"I'm here!" I cried out. "I'm here! Just hold on! Help is coming!"

"I can't...move...my legs," he whispered.

I forced myself to look away from his bloody face to scan the rest of his body. His seatbelt was pulled taut across his chest and abdomen, clearly making it harder for him to breathe. The roof was slightly caved in, forcing his head to tilt at an incredibly awkward angle. I couldn't tell from my vantage point what the front of the car looked like, but I could visibly see that the engine was pressing against the dashboard, pinning Alec's long legs beneath the heavy debris.

He glanced up at me with a look of utter desperation as he struggled to lift his arm.

I leaned over, careful not to dislodge the car in any way, and took his hand. His trembling fingers felt like ice.

At that moment, I could hear the sirens wailing in the distance.

"Do you hear that?" I asked him. "Help is almost here. You just hold on a little longer, okay? Keep talking to me!"

"Hard...to breathe..."

I gave his hand a gentle squeeze. "I know, babe. But I need you to stay alert. Just keep your eyes on me." My tear-filled eyes temporarily blurred the horrific image in front of me, but I blinked them away to keep my focus on Alec's hopeless stare.

"I'm...sorry," he whispered. "I was...coming...to see..."

"I know..." I whimpered. "Don't worry about that right now."

The minutes that passed before the Rescue Squad arrived seemed to take forever. Every second felt like an hour, especially given the fact that Alec's breathing was becoming shallower and shallower, and he was not talking as much.

~*~*~*~

I found myself standing beside my dad as the Firefighters and EMTs worked to stabilize the car with some metal struts and small airbags so that they could attempt to reach Alec without causing further injury to him, or themselves.

What was making me extra nervous was the fact that I had not heard a single sound come from Alec since I was forced to leave my perch on the huge rock.

When I had to walk away, I felt as if my lifeline to him had been severed.

I know that probably sounds insane, but it's the only way I could describe how I was feeling.

I watched an EMT immediately hook Alec up to an IV through the huge hole where the front windshield should have been.

Then a Fireman hopped up on the boulder where I once stood and leaned over the side of the car. "Hey, my man. My name's Rich. How're ya holding up?"

I didn't hear Alec reply, but I assumed that he had because Fireman Rich kept talking.

"I know, bud. We got the car stabilized now, so we're gonna get you outta there, but first, you're gonna hear some loud noises while the Jaws of Life cut out an opening so we can reach you. Alright?" Rich nodded as if responding to something Alec had said. "That's right. I'm gonna drape a sheet above you, so nothing falls on you while we work. Just hang tight." Rich then turned back to one of his men. "Okay, Jesse. You're good to go."

Fireman Jesse picked up a sizeable claw-like machine and walked around to the other side of the car.

"Stay to your left once you get to the driver's side, Jesse," Rich told him. "His head is pressing against the roof."

An ominous rumble of thunder resounded in the distance,

which caused both men to stare at each other for longer than I was comfortable with.

"Put a rush on it," Rich added. "I wanna have him outta here before this storm hits. But be careful!"

The two men nodded at each other one more time. Then the sound of a small engine reverberated in my ears, followed by the crunching and screeching of metal on metal.

In no time at all, the jaws had cut away all four connecting points of the roof.

Rich knelt down and removed whatever sheet he had used to cover Alec's face. "You're doing great, my man. Just a few more minutes." Then Rich jumped down and jogged over to where Jesse was standing.

Three more Firemen joined them. Rich positioned himself so that he could see Alec; then he guided the other men as they slowly and meticulously removed the roof.

As soon as they were safely out of the way, the EMTs quickly moved in. One stabilized Alec's neck with a brace; the another placed a small backboard between him and the driver's seat to stabilize his back in case of a spinal injury.

By that point, it had started sprinkling. The entire time they were working on him, I could not stop crying. And just when I thought the nightmare was almost over, I overheard Rich explaining to Alec that they were going to use some more airbags to lift the front portion of the car from his legs so that he could be removed from the wreckage. But if his circulation was compromised, then once the debris was removed, and his blood was able to circulate again, the process was going to be very painful.

Once the airbags were placed, Rich explained everything again to Alec, making sure he understood exactly what was about to happen.

I listened to the generator as it started to pump air through the small lines to the airbag. I heard a cracking sound as the heavy engine and the twisted metal were slowly lifted away.

At first, everything seemed fine, but then the woods were suddenly filled with Alec's screams.

Agonizingly, high-pitched, tortured screams.

The Firefighters and EMTs painstakingly removed Alec from the remnants of his car, securing him to a backboard for the long trek back up the hill to the awaiting ambulance.

An oxygen mask was placed over his mouth and nose while his flailing arms were strapped down.

Amidst the commotion and chaos, Alec's bloodshot eyes locked onto mine. He was screaming my name over and over, followed by, "I'm sorry."

I could not see anything by that point. My eyes knew only tears and blurred vision.

CHAPTER 20

Just after Alec was loaded into the back of the ambulance, the skies opened up. I was ushered into the passenger seat, and the door was slammed shut behind me.

"We gotta get going!" the EMT in the back called out. "His heart rate is skyrocketing, and his limbs are starting to swell!"

"I'm on it!" the other one replied. The driver jumped behind the wheel and revved the engine before racing down the road at breakneck speed.

The siren blaring overhead alerted all the other vehicles on the road to let us pass.

Even though we were only a ten to twenty-minute drive from the hospital, the ride there seemed to be endless; made even worse by the torrential downpour that was continuing to flood the streets.

The rain was coming down in thick sheets, pitter-pattering on the windshield. I tried to focus on the squeaky wiper blades going back and forth, but all the while, Alec was screaming and struggling against the restraints in the back.

I wanted to turn around. I wanted to hold his hand. I wanted to tell him that everything was going to be okay. But I knew that if I laid eyes on him, I would lose what little composure I had left. And I needed to be strong…for the both of us.

As we pulled into the emergency drop-off lane, I heard the words *hypotension, renal failure, acidosis, hyperkalemia,* and *hypocalcemia* coming out of the EMTs' mouths as they shouted back and forth, but I had no idea what any of those things meant.

It wasn't until I overheard one of them say, "He has some cranial damage to the front of his face…" that I felt the need to interject.

"He has Treacher Collins Syndrome," I told them. "There's nothing wrong with his face…other than the gash on his forehead."

The two men glanced up at me with puzzled expressions for half a second before turning their attention back to their patient.

Moments later, we stopped in front of the emergency area of the hospital. A group of doctors and nurses were waiting at the entrance. The EMTs continued to yell over Alec's screams, relaying his stats and injuries as he was quickly wheeled away.

I tried to follow, but I was stopped at the swinging double doors.

~ ONLY MEDICAL PERSONNEL BEYOND THIS POINT ~

I peered through the small rectangular window until Alec was out of sight…though his screams took longer to fade away.

I asked one of the nurses if I could use the phone. I dialed Liza's number so that I could let her know what was going on.

As the line started to ring, I planned on asking her to get in touch with Brock so that he could let Alec's family know what had happened, but when she answered the phone, I could not seem to form any coherent words. I began crying so hard that I could not catch my breath.

I felt my dad's hand on my shoulder as he gently took the phone from my trembling hands. "Hello, Liza…yes, we found him…no…no, it's not good…"

Another sob forced its way out of my body as I turned and headed toward the waiting area. I didn't want to listen to the phone call. I couldn't bear to relive all those details again.

~*~*~*~

A few hours later, I heard a familiar voice asking about Alec.

My exhausted gaze landed on Lindy, Henry, and Cora, lingering near the nurses' station.

I stood, causing my dad to glance my way. "Everything okay, sweetheart?"

I shook my head and swallowed, unable to stop the tears that were threatening to come back full force.

He followed my gaze and took my hand, giving it a squeeze. "I'll talk to them."

I nodded, unable to move.

My dad made his way over, casually making a conversation with the people that were so close, yet so far from me.

Both of his parents looked my way. The concerned expressions and vacant stares on their faces broke my heart all over again. And when Lindy smiled at me half-heartedly, my tears escaped in a violent stream.

Both Lindy and Cora came over and wrapped their arms around me. That seemingly sweet gesture was my undoing. I ultimately fell apart right there in the waiting room in their embrace.

The three of us stood there crying, holding onto one another as if the world was going to end at any moment.

"Has there been any news?" I heard Henry ask.

"No, they won't tell us anything because we're not family," my dad replied.

"Well, as soon as we know anything, I promise we will let you and Scarlett know." Henry shook my dad's hand.

"Thank you," my dad said quietly.

I finally managed to pry myself out of the small group hug. "This is all my fault," I whimpered.

Lindy wiped the tears from my face and kissed my cheek. "Shhh, Scarlett, no. No, honey, none of this is your fault."

"But if I had just listened to him…if I had just let him explain…then he wouldn't have been driving up here…and he wouldn't be…"

Lindy pulled me back in for a hug. "Couples fight…and then they make up. Things happen that are out of our control, but you must have faith that something better is just around the corner."

I glanced up at her through tears, remembering the words that Alec had told me only a few short weeks ago when I had asked about his tattoo. *To have the strength to overcome life's obstacles, you first must have faith that something better is just around the corner.*

"This situation will strengthen you both," Lindy told me. She sniffled and sighed as a small smile crept across her lips. "Alec is a fighter. Always has been."

I smiled at her words. "Yeah, he is."

A nurse dressed in dark blue scrubs made her way over and cleared her throat. "Mr. and Mrs. Cavanaugh?"

All of our attention was instantly shifted in her direction.

The nurse held her clipboard tighter against her chest and put on a professional smile. "I need Alec's family to come with me, please."

Lindy squeezed my hands, and I squeezed right back. We nodded at each other, and then she followed her husband and her daughter down the long hallway through the double doors that separated me from the man who may very well be the love of my life.

CHAPTER 21

Alec was in surgery for over sixteen hours. Something none of us expected.

Lindy and Henry continued to give me updates, but most of the time they were too distraught to say anything with too much detail.

Alec's forehead needed fifty-seven stitches – he had a pretty severe concussion – a few of his ribs were cracked, but thankfully none were broken – there was some extensive damage to his legs from being pinned beneath the engine for so long, so the doctors were still working on him…

The last few times Lindy came out to the waiting room, she let me know that Alec was still alive, nothing more.

At some point, I must have fallen asleep because my dad started shaking me, muttering something about Alec's condition.

I immediately bolted upright, wiping the lingering drool from my chin, frantically looking around to get my bearings. "What's happened? What's going on?"

"Alec has finally come out of surgery," my dad told me. "His mother just came out to give us an update. He's alive, but he's in critical condition. His stats still haven't gotten any better."

My heart dropped. "You don't think he's going to…?" I just could not bring myself to say the last word.

My dad shook his head and shrugged slightly. "I don't know, sweetheart. I just don't know." He wrapped his arms around my shoulders. "All we can do right now is say a prayer to the Big Man upstairs and have faith that Alec will be alright."

~*~*~*~

Four days passed before I was finally allowed to see Alec. So, in the span of ninety-six intense hours, which I had spent in and out of the ER waiting room, I didn't sleep for more than a few minutes at a time. I was a mixture of excited, exhausted, and nervous.

As a nurse led me down the hall, everyone on that floor seemed to be on edge, and no one was giving me too much detail as to what was going on. I chalked it up to the emotional turmoil of the past few days, but when I saw Lindy pacing outside a closed door with a distressed expression on her face, my heart constricted in my chest.

When she noticed me, her eyes widened, and she stopped walking. A single tear slid down her cheek. She wiped her eyes and sniffled as she welcomed me with a hug. "He's doing much better today." She sniffled again. "The doctors say that his electrolytes have finally stabilized and that against all odds, his kidney function and heart rate have returned to a more normal range…but…"

Suddenly, there was a loud commotion coming from the door beside us. Lindy didn't finish her sentence. Instead, she rushed inside, and I followed behind her. We were greeted by a flying plastic pitcher full of ice. We both ducked as the frozen shrapnel flew past. I yelped involuntarily as a few pieces of ice hit my arm.

Alec's blood-shot eyes automatically locked onto mine.

I smiled, expecting the same thing in return…instead, he

started shouting and cursing and throwing more objects. The roll-away table that was holding his food was shoved away so hard that his tray and drink spilled all over the floor.

"GET HER THE HELL OUT OF HERE!" he yelled. "I TOLD YOU I DON'T WANT TO SEE HER! I DON'T WANT TO SEE ANYONE!"

I jumped back, rushing out of the room just as a handful of plastic utensils were thrown my way. I stood there in shock as Alec's words became muffled by the closed door.

A second or so later, Lindy joined me in the hallway. "I'm so sorry," she said softly. "He hasn't been himself since the accident. He's only been coherent for the last day and a half, and he isn't taking things well. One second he is literally begging us to let you see him, and then the next, he is pleading with us to keep you away. I just don't…"

"Does he have brain damage?" I blurted out, not meaning to interrupt her.

She shook her head. "No, Scarlett." Then she sighed and placed her hand on my shoulder. "Why don't we take a walk…"

We strolled side by side down the empty hallway. The sound of ventilators and heart monitors filled the silence until she finally spoke.

"I think my son is in love with you," she whispered.

My breath caught in my throat, and my feet suddenly stopped moving on their own accord.

Lindy stopped too and turned to face me. "I'm not sure if those exact words have ever been spoken between the two of you, but I've seen my son blossom into a whole new person after you came into his life." She sighed. "He was always such a sweet little boy. He never talked back, always did his chores, rarely ever complained about anything…but those bullies…"

We were nearly at the end of the hallway, so she gestured toward an empty waiting room. I sat beside her as she continued.

"Alec hasn't had the easiest life. We tried to give him everything he could ever need, but the world isn't the wonderful, forgiving, accepting place that we wish it was for our children." She glanced my way and touched my arm. "He found his safe place with you. And now…now he's…" Her words trailed off, and she sighed again while shaking her head sadly.

"It doesn't seem like I'm his safe place. Not with him throwing things at me and screaming at me to get out of his room." I stared down at my hands and nervously played with my fingers. "He's lashed out at me once before. And he promised it would never happen again."

Lindy sighed deeply. "I apologize on his behalf, Scarlett. Alec has lost a part of himself because of this accident. He doesn't feel like the man he once was. He's just scared."

A few minutes passed before I found my voice again. "Scared of what?"

Her reply was immediate. "That you'll walk away once you know…"

Before either of us could say anything else, an elderly couple stepped into the room and sat on the opposite side. With our privacy compromised, Lindy cleared her throat and stood. I followed suit, and we headed back down the hall toward Alec's room.

Neither of us said anything while we stood in front of his door once again. Not much time had passed since Alec's freak-out-moment, so I was more than a little apprehensive about stepping foot back inside.

Lindy placed her hand on the handle and looked me in the eye. "I have never overstepped boundaries with my children; I want you to know that…but I can't let my only son…my baby boy…" Her voice cracked as her eyes filled with tears. Then she sighed and regained her composure. "Give me two minutes, and you will be able to talk to him."

What was I supposed to say to that?

Alec clearly didn't want to see me. His actions a short

while ago proved that, so I didn't respond. I just stood there staring at her until she opened the door and shut it gently behind her.

Almost instantly, voices were raised and arguing promptly ensued. Both Lindy and Henry, as well as Cora and Alec, were all shouting at each other. The four of them were all talking over one another. And I felt like I was intruding on some private moment, but I didn't dare move.

A few seconds later, it was silent again. The handle on the door jiggled, and Henry appeared in the doorway with Lindy and Cora close behind. He gave me a heartfelt nod as he walked away.

Cora stepped closer and pulled me in for an unexpected hug.

Lastly, Lindy squeezed my shoulder and kissed my cheek. "Just be honest with him, dear," she said. "Whatever he asks, just tell him the truth. Even if it hurts."

My brow furrowed in a confused fashion as she headed down the hall, disappearing around the corner with the rest of her family. I stood there in the opened doorway, not really understanding the situation I had found myself in.

I took a peek inside. The curtain was pulled, so I couldn't see Alec from where I was standing; which made me relax for a second because that meant that he couldn't see me either.

I swallowed down my doubts and stepped inside, closing the door behind me. The discernible click was followed by his voice.

"Scarlett?"

"The one and only," I replied quietly.

He sighed.

"Can I come in, or…?"

Sigh number two escaped his lips. "Not yet."

"Okay…" I stood there awkwardly, shifting my weight from one leg to the other, waiting for *not yet* to be over.

Sigh number three…four…

"Alec…what in the world is going on?" I finally choked out. "Why don't you want to see me? It's like our first meeting all over again! What is the secret this time?"

Sigh number five. "It's just one more flaw to add to the list. I just… I don't…" Sigh number six.

"*Alec*," I growled. "Start making some sense or I'm coming around this damn curtain with or without your permission!"

Sigh number seven. "They took my fucking legs," he blurted out. "I don't have my…"

He didn't have time to say anything else. I rushed past the curtain to stare into his saddened and terrified eyes.

There were small cuts and scrapes covering his beautiful face, and one of his eyes was heavily bruised, as well as most of his lower jaw. Not to mention the stitches across his forehead.

The beeping on the heart monitor suddenly skyrocketed as he glanced down at the bed, then his gaze locked back on mine.

My eyes took in the rest of him, lingering on the blanket where both of his long legs should have been. Instead, nearly half of the bed was flat.

Trembling sigh number eight escaped his lips. "Double amputation. Just below the knee." His voice was seemingly void of any emotion, and his eyes were vacant and glassy as if he was not comprehending the words coming out of his own mouth. "The doctors described my condition as 'crush syndrome'." He scoffed. "Another damn syndrome." He paused again. "Since my legs were pinned for so long, the blood stopped circulating…and basically…my extremities…died."

The shock seemed to have taken away my ability to speak, so I just continued to stare. I honestly don't know what I was expecting…but it sure as hell wasn't that.

"It's just one more flaw," he muttered. "One more thing to disfigure me. One more ugly scar to…"

"STOP IT!" I shouted. My tears were starting to build all over again. "Just stop it!"

The door unexpectedly opened, and a nurse stepped in to check on him. She apologized for the intrusion and quickly excused herself once she was done.

"You're being ridiculous," I stated as I shook my head. "Absolutely ridiculous…not to mention irrational!"

His vacant stare seemed to disappear as he angrily jerked the blanket away, revealing the bandaged stumps that were once his long, muscular, tanned legs. "THIS IS RIDICULOUS AND IRRATIONAL?" His words came out high-pitched and frantic, nothing like his usually deep and steady voice.

I wanted to tell him that what I *meant* by those words, was that I was glad he had survived no matter what the outcome had been. I wanted to let him know that I shared in his distress and that I was so sorry for what he had lost. But in the end, I was just happy that he was alive. I didn't contemplate anything past that. But when he started shouting at me, everything going through my mind instantly scattered. So, I just stood there, still shaking my head as tears streamed down my face.

"Just. Get. Out!" he seethed.

"What?" I asked unbelievably.

"You heard me."

"Alec, that's not what I meant…"

"JUST SHUT UP!" he shouted at me. "And get out."

My mouth fell open.

He began breathing heavily as his jaw tightened. Then the heart monitor started rising higher and higher. When he spoke again, his mocking tone sent a dagger through my heart. "I don't need your false hope and your petty sympathy, Scarlett! In fact, I don't need you here! I don't want you here! So, for the love of God, STOP STARING AT ME LIKE I'M SOME KIND OF FREAK, AND GET THE HELL OUT OF MY ROOM! GET THE HELL

AWAY FROM ME!"

I covered my shock-ridden face and burst into full-blown tears. I ran out of the room just as two nurses were on their way in. I passed by Henry and Lindy who were standing at the nurses' station a short distance away.

"Scarlett? Scarlett, what happened?" they called out.

I ignored both of their voices calling my name as I threw open the door at the end of the hall and raced down the stairs.

CHAPTER 22

The very next morning, I woke up to a light tapping on my bedroom door. I groggily sat up, rubbing my tired swollen eyes. "Yeah?" I yawned as I spoke.

My dad came into my room and gestured back toward the hall. "You have a visitor."

I gave him a questioning stare, but he didn't give me any other information before he walked away.

I blew out an irritated sigh and lugged myself out of my warm and comfy bed. I threw my hair up in a ponytail and then headed down the stairs, taking them two at a time like I used to do when I was a kid.

At the bottom landing, I came face to face with Alec's sister, Cora. Her expression was unreadable as she stood silently in my parents' living room.

An emotional lump abruptly lodged itself in my throat, and my stomach filled itself with nervous butterflies.

She clasped her hands in front of her and bit her bottom lip. "Hi, Scarlett. Can we speak for a minute? Privately."

I lingered on the bottom step with my hand still clutching the banister.

I guess she could sense my hesitation, because a few seconds later she said, "Please? It's important."

"Is Alec alright?" I asked.

She sighed in response. "That's a complicated question...with an even more complex answer. Which is why I came to talk to you."

"Okay," I finally said. I led her out to the front porch. I sat down on the swing, and she opted for the small space beside me.

Cora didn't speak right away. Instead, she sighed while we gently swayed back and forth.

Curiosity and anticipation were literally eating me alive while the silence between us continued to stretch on.

Cora placed her foot on the porch floor to stop the swing from moving. Another sigh escaped her mouth, but it sounded much more tortured than the last. That was when I noticed the tears silently making their way down her cheeks.

"I think my brother is slowly losing his mind," she whispered. "After you left, he started lashing out at everyone and everything in his reach. I've never seen him act like that in my whole life. He was...going crazy." She paused and sniffled before continuing. "He ripped out his IV line and then he threw the blood pressure cuff across the room. He even managed to knock over the heavy machinery beside his bed before he tried to get up unassisted...which resulted in his stitches ripping open on both of his legs." Cora paused again to wipe her eyes. "The doctors had to rush him back into surgery."

I reflexively grabbed Cora's hand. "Oh, my God! Please tell me that he's going to be alright."

She squeezed my hand. "I honestly don't know how to answer that. He was screaming and shouting and crying while the nurses struggled to restrain him. It eventually took five huge male nurses to hold my baby brother down so he could be taken back to the operating room." She stopped speaking again as a sob nearly choked her. "Since then, he's been sedated…for his own protection." She swallowed and sighed before shifting her body so that she was fully facing me. "I know what he said to you, Scarlett."

I glanced in her direction.

"I didn't mean to eavesdrop. I just happened to be standing in earshot of the door when he started yelling." Her big brown eyes were pleading for me to understand. "I know this whole situation has been hard on you as well…but please, I need you to come back to the hospital. I know he didn't mean what he said…as horrible as it was. That was just the fear talking. My brother may seem like he's got it all figured out…like he's got his whole life together…but the truth is, he's scared shitless about all this. Waking up to find your body mutilated…to find out that parts of you are literally missing…I can't even begin to imagine what that would be like. But I think if he sees you when he wakes up again, it will make him realize that everything will be okay. That even after losing both of his legs…he will be okay."

I blinked away unwanted tears of my own. "I don't know, Cora. What if he still doesn't want to see me? Or worse, what if me being there makes him freak out all over again?"

She stood, pulling me up with her. "Look, my brother is stubborn, not stupid. He knows he messed up. And if he acts like a jackass again, I'll put him in his place." She made a fist and flexed. "I can take him."

I found myself unconsciously smiling as a soft laugh escaped. "Alright," I agreed. "I'll give it one more shot."

~*~*~*~

I waited outside of Alec's room while Cora headed in to inform her parents that she had convinced me to come back.

Almost instantly, Lindy appeared in the doorway. She took me in her arms and squeezed me so tight that it was actually hard to breathe. "Thank you," she whispered. "Thank you for coming back."

A familiar nurse stepped out of Alec's room and placed her hand on Lindy's shoulder. "The sedation is wearing off, ma'am. He will be waking up shortly."

"Thank you," Lindy replied quietly.

As the nurse walked away, she gave me what I could only describe as 'the stink-eye'.

Great...the staff must think that I am the cause of all this mayhem.

Lindy turned back to me, derailing my thoughts. "He's been restrained...as a precaution...you know, because of what happened last time. I just want you to be prepared for that."

I swallowed that stupid nervous lump that always seemed to be in my throat and followed her into Alec's room.

As the door clicked shut, I heard Henry talking quietly to Alec. "Just take it easy, son. No, no. You're okay. No, the doctor was able to... Yes, it's alright. I know it hurts. Just hold still. Alec! You have to stay calm, or they will sedate you again!"

The heart monitor started going crazy.

"ALEC, CALM DOWN!" Cora shouted.

I rushed around the curtain and locked eyes with Alec just as three nurses rushed in.

"Everything is fine," Henry assured them. "He just...had a little moment of panic when he first woke up, but he's alright now." He glanced back to his son. "Right?"

Alec nodded without taking his wide eyes off me.

The oxygen mask on his face fogged up and cleared quickly, showing how rapid his breathing was coming and going.

The nurses were not taking any chances. They checked Alec's vitals and gave him a quick once-over.

I heard one of them whisper to Henry as she passed by, "If this happens again, he will be sedated, and you will all be asked to leave. This is the ICU; there are very sick patients here. We can't have outbursts like this. He needs a calm atmosphere to heal."

When the nurse finally made her exit, that was when I

noticed that Lindy was still standing by the opened door. "Let's give Alec a few minutes alone with Scarlett," she stated firmly. Then she ushered her family out of the room without giving any of them time to object. Before she closed the door, she smiled in my direction and offered me a simple nod.

I stood at the end of Alec's bed, feeling more than a little uncomfortable, and completely unsure of what to do.

"You came back," he mumbled through the mask.

"Cora asked me to," I replied quietly, avoiding his burning stare.

From the corner of my eye, I saw his expression turn sad. "I'm sorry, Scarlett…"

It was the tears falling down his face that made me finally decide to move closer.

"Alec…what do you want out of all this?" I gestured between the two of us. "Because you are always angry about something…or you're trying to hide from me in some way."

Much to my surprise, he didn't look away. "Can you please move this damn mask so I can talk normally?"

For a split second, I had forgotten all about him being unable to move. "Uh…am I allowed to do that?"

He struggled against the restraints that were holding him to the bed. "I'd do it myself, but I'm a little tied up at the moment."

I smiled. "Smart ass."

He let out a deep sigh as I removed the piece of plastic from his face and wiped a tear from his cheek. "Thank you," he whispered.

"If you start to hyperventilate, you only have yourself to blame."

He flashed me his perfect smile, which I had not seen in weeks. "I'll be fine."

"Uh huh."

Alec sighed and glanced down at the leather restraints that were around his wrists and upper thighs. "How ridiculous do I look right now?"

I was not sure if he used that particular word on purpose because of our last encounter, so I decided to try to lighten the mood. "You look like you belong in an insane asylum," I joked.

I expected Alec to laugh, or at least crack a smile, but he didn't. Instead, he looked heartbroken.

Well, shit.

The same words he said to me the last time we were face to face came out of his mouth. "It's just one more flaw."

"You seriously need to stop talking like that! From the first moment I met you, all you've been doing is trying to hide things that you consider flaws...to keep me from seeing the real you." I took a step closer and slowly pulled back the blanket. Which was probably a real asshole move, considering that Alec could not stop me in his current state.

"Scarlett, don't! Please!" He started to struggle.

I worried that he was going to tear his stitches again, so I got right in his face. "DAMMIT, ALEC! IF THIS IS GONNA WORK BETWEEN US, YOU'VE GOT TO STOP HIDING FROM ME!"

The heart monitor was starting to climb again. And Alec's lips twitched as his eyes began to water. I could see some anger there, too...but he did eventually stop moving.

I stood there breathing heavily as if I had just run some marathon. Alec was doing the same.

Forcing him to lie there, as I gawked at his recently amputated limbs, while he was literally tied to the bed, seemed a bit too cruel and disturbing...and just plain wrong. So, I unhooked each cuff on his wrists and then sat on the edge of the mattress with my back to him.

I could feel him shifting behind me and then he leaned his head against my shoulder. "I don't think I can do this, Scarlett."

"Yes, you can," I assured him. "You're so much stronger than you think."

He sighed heavily. "No, I'm not talking about my legs. I'm trying here…I really am trying to make this work. I'm trying to stay strong, but I can't keep pretending that what we have isn't going to fall apart someday and blow up in my face. It's inevitable."

His whispered words caught me off guard as I turned around in surprise. "What?" My mouth was hanging open in complete disbelief as I pulled away from him. "What the hell are you talking about, Alec?"

His brilliant blue eyes stared at me, seemingly void of the love that had always shown through. "This is all just too much to deal with. And I just don't know if we…" He shook his head and briefly looked away. "I think we will both be better off in the long run if things just end right here."

"End?" I repeated. Then I mimicked his head shake. "No! You don't mean that! You're talking crazy!"

Alec let out a soft laugh while tears filled his eyes. "This isn't me being impulsive, Scarlett. I've thought a lot about it. And this is the honesty that you deserve. The man that I was when I was with you before…is gone. There is no need to try to make something work that is destined for failure. We had fun. You can at least admit that to yourself. But c'mon…did you really expect us to run off into the sunset, get married, and have a family someday?" He glanced down at his legs. "I mean, look at me…there will be no running for this man. There is no sunset on the horizon."

I leapt off the bed and took a few steps away. "Don't say that! You will get better. You will heal. It just takes time. Let me be there for you. Let me help you get through this!"

His eyes were shimmering when he finally looked my way again. "I don't want you to help me, Scarlett. Don't you understand what I'm trying to tell you?"

A soft sob caught in my throat. "Don't do this," I told him. My voice cracked on the last word.

"Don't beg to be with me," he whimpered. "That's not who you are."

I made a little hiccup sound as I tried to hold back my tears. "You're going to come to your senses and realize that you're making a mistake!" I cried out. "You're going to realize that you were just letting your fear control you! Just give it some time and let us figure it all out together..."

Alec sighed deeply and looked away again. "You don't have a clue what I'm going through! So, please stop standing there with your 'it's not so bad, we can get through this together' attitude! It's not *we* that has to get through this...it's *me*! Last I checked, you still had both of your legs!"

I felt like my entire life was falling apart right in front of my eyes and I was helpless to stop it. My breath exhaled in a shudder as my tears started to fall. "You must have brain damage! You would never say these things to me otherwise!"

His piercing stare seemed to bore a hole into the depths of my soul. "Don't make this any harder than it already is. Just turn around and walk away. Don't look back."

I covered my face as I burst into tears. "You wanted me back here! So, why are you trying to make me go again?"

"I couldn't leave things the way I did, so I wanted to see you one last time...to end things right. Please just walk away, Scarlett...and don't come back. No matter what my family may tell you, I won't ask to see you again."

I stood there staring at him, my entire body trembling from head to toe. My heart was sinking in my chest, and my stomach was twisting and churning. "Are you sure this is what you want?" I choked out. "Because I will wait for you. If you just need some time..."

He didn't respond. In fact, he didn't even look at me again. Instead, he sighed and leaned back in his bed, turning away from me.

Silence was the answer he gave me. A deafening silence so loud that my ears began to ache.

He really didn't want me anymore.

After everything we had gone through…after everything we had overcome…he wanted things to end…just like that.

I slowly turned around, struggling to retain my composure. I hesitated at the door, pausing with my hand on the handle. I glanced back over my shoulder. Alec still had his face turned away, looking out the window.

When I stepped out into the hall, a crushing weight settled within my chest. I saw Alec's family a short distance away at the end of the corridor, but I could not bear to face them. So, I ran in the opposite direction and took the back stairs…just like last time.

CHAPTER 23

As I raced through the opened double doors at the front entrance of the hospital, my self-control finally reached zero. A bloodcurdling scream erupted from my throat, as if it had been caged and waiting for that perfect moment of release.

Almost immediately, I heard a commotion coming from behind me. In my peripheral vision, I could see multiple patients and staff quickly approaching. But before they could get to me, I took off running across the parking lot.

I didn't know where I was headed, nor did I care; I just wanted to get as far away from that damn hospital as possible.

With the warm sun drying my tear-stained face, I mindlessly managed to travel the full ten miles back to my parents' cabin. By the time I had arrived, I physically could not stand anymore, and my swollen eyes were unable to produce any more tears.

When I walked through the front door, both of my parents were waiting for me with concerned expressions covering their faces.

My mom was the first to come up and give me a much-needed hug. "Where have you been, sweetheart? What happened? Lindy has been calling every few minutes for the last couple hours. And your dad was out looking for you!"

Just as I was about to open my mouth, the phone started to ring.

My dad walked over and picked up the receiver. "Hello?" He paused and glanced my way. "Yes, she just made it home. She's safe." Another pause as he lowered his voice. "No, we haven't had a chance to talk to her. I don't know. Yes, I will. Okay, Lindy. Bye for now."

Both of my parents stood there staring at me with questions lingering in their eyes.

"Alec and I..." my whispered words nearly choked me. "...he...he broke up with me. So, I left...and I ran...I ran the whole way here...but I..."

My mom didn't wait for me to finish. Instead, she pulled me back into her arms. "Oh, sweetheart, I am so sorry!"

Of course, my tears managed to come back full force.

My dad wrapped his arms around both my mom and me. "I'm sure he didn't mean it, honey. He'll come around. Let Lindy talk to him; I'm sure she will be able..."

"I DON'T WANNA THINK ABOUT IT ANYMORE!" I shouted, intentionally interrupting him. Then, before either of them had a chance to say anything else, I tore myself away and ran up the stairs.

I slammed my bedroom door and locked it behind me before collapsing onto my bed. My emotional state completely crumbled as I clutched my chest and began gasping for air.

I realized in that moment what the term 'heartbreak' actually meant. A sob forced its way from my mouth as I curled up into a fetal position.

My heart was literally in pain. A physical reaction that I was not prepared for.

The throbbing ache seemed to take over my entire body, spreading to my limbs, and thrusting me into a depression so deep that I feared I would never be free.

It was as if I was on a rollercoaster, being pulled this way and that…feeling the butterflies turn into nausea…wishing desperately that the ride would end.

~*~*~*~

For the next three days, I rarely left my room.

Lindy called at least twice during the day, and multiple times throughout the night…though I never did speak with her.

When I got back home, the pattern continued; the only difference being, that Liza was the one taking down Lindy's messages.

I could not for the life of me verbally express myself without bursting into tears. That was when Liza suggested that I try my hand at writing some poetry. As it turned out, that was exactly what I needed to release some of the painful pressure building up inside me.

Once upon a time, I used to be your world...

Once upon a time, I used to be your girl...

Once upon a time, you used to take my calls...

Once upon a time, we used to have it all...

I wish I could forget you and believe me I've tried.

I can't begin to count all the tears that I've cried.

But your face never leaves me, and your voice haunts my dreams.

I feel like I'm trapped in a nightmare where nothing is as it seems.

You called me your soulmate, the other half of your heart...

Yet, I'm left screaming in vain while I'm falling apart.

I know you can hear me...you know I'm in pain...

But you still leave me here crying all alone in the rain.

Maybe you'll miss me...maybe you won't.

Maybe you love me...maybe you don't.

What could have been is what used to be.

What we have now feels like I'm lost at sea...

Constantly pulled deep down under the waves

Struggling for a breath that only you can save.

So, I'll keep waiting for your call, or a message, or clue

That maybe there is still some remnants of you.

<u>CHAPTER 24</u>

Christmas and the New Year came and went, and I felt no cheer whatsoever.

I could not tell you how many times Liza had burst into my room in the middle of the night, only to find me sobbing uncontrollably, struggling to catch my breath.

Losing Alec had sparked an emotional breakdown that I never would have expected. Everything inside of me hurt…and every day it seemed to be getting worse. And not like a scrape or a bruise that would heal with time; this was a deep, grief-stricken, misery-ridden ache that seemed to be spreading throughout my body. It latched onto every microscopic inch of me…taking over every muscle, every bone, every vein…until the only thing holding me together was pain.

Every night, I asked the same question…sometimes out loud, sometimes just to myself. Poor Liza, she did her best to console me.

"Why is he doing this?" I choked out. "Why did he leave me?"

My best friend wrapped her arms around my trembling

body and rocked me back and forth like a child, stroking my hair and rubbing my back. "Sometimes people do stupid things." She sighed, "I wish I had a better answer for you, my lovely. I really do."

"But…I thought…I thought he loved me…" Another round of sobs took over my body.

Liza squeezed me tighter. "Shhh. It's gonna be okay. I promise this feeling won't last forever."

And luckily for me, she was right.

Over the next six months, my life was slowly getting back to normal…but let me tell you, it was one hell of a ride.

Many sleepless, tear-filled nights were spent listening to 'Nothing Compares 2 U' by Sinead O'Connor on repeat…screaming into my pillow until my throat was raw…feeling like my heart was being ripped apart inside my chest.

Ice-cream, plus romantic comedies, soon equaled our new break-up ritual. And boy, could I consume a tub of mint chocolate chip!

Eventually, the throbbing sensation that had been strangling my heart began to fade. Little by little, pieces of my former self began to return. I was finally able to smile without it being forced, and laughter was no longer a thing of the past.

During the healing process, Liza suggested that I write Alec one of my poems, or a letter, or both. She said that I should pour my heart out to him, and then burn it to release all the negative energy that was still buried inside me. I remember scoffing at her and rolling my eyes at such a silly idea…but after thinking about it for a few days, I ended up sitting down at my desk and letting the words spill out.

Alec…I still see your face.

Your familiar face that somehow continues to haunt my dreams.

I relive all those days we spent together.

Of the fantasy life...the one I wish I could live again.

I knew your name.

It rolled off my lips, causing butterflies to start fluttering in my stomach.

I knew your smile.

It lit up my life like the sun creeping over the horizon.

And I knew your laugh.

The sound filled my soul with a joy that I had never known.

Now...everything is different.

You're gone.

The laughter is gone.

But the pain remains.

Your familiar ways are now foreign.

Why did you change?

Where did you go?

Your once gentle words are now harsh, empty whispers of the past that are still ringing in my ears.

My mind continues to cling to what's left of you, while my heart still aches at the thought of you.

Just the mention of your name...

Or hearing a song we once played...

They bring back such beautiful memories, but leave a hole in my chest.

The worst part is...you're not here.

I can see you clearly in my mind, but I can never touch you.

You know that feeling you get when you see someone after a long time has passed...

That sick, nervous feeling that almost feels good?

I hate that.

I really hate that.

But for some reason, I don't hate you.

Why do you continue to make me feel this way even after all this time?

I haven't spoken to you in months, yet you still have this hold on me.

It hurts.

Every day it hurts.

But that pain only proves that what we had was real.

I miss you.

I miss us.

But I will get better...that's all you need to know.

I placed my pencil back on my desk and wiped my eyes while I stared at what I had just written. Then I reached for the pack of matches beside my cluster of candles. I struck the head on the little strip, watching as the fire danced between my fingers. As I slowly brought it closer to the corner of the sheet, I hesitated, but only for a second. When the fire finally kissed the paper, the orange flames quickly spread over the words...my words...for him...curling and charring their edges, before engulfing them completely.

I carefully placed the burning remnants into a small metal trash can and watched until my written feelings became nothing but little black specks. I wiped my eyes again and took a deep breath. That act had been much more emotional than I had expected. As the final smoldering pieces burned out, I closed my eyes and pictured Alec's beautiful face.

It was really over.

~*~*~*~

The next two months, I was in what I could only describe as zombie-mode. I went to work, and I came home, with the occasional eating in between.

One Friday afternoon, I was resting on the couch after a long day. My head was leaned back, and my eyes were closed. And for the first time in a long time, I wasn't thinking about Alec. I was thinking about how much my feet hurt and how tired I was.

A couple weeks prior I had received a promotion…one that I was all too happy to take. The downside was that I was exhausted every single day when I got home. The upside, however, was that I had less and less time to obsess over Alec. Just as I was about to doze off, I heard Liza's voice coming from the kitchen.

"You got a letter in the mail today," she informed me. "I almost threw it away, but then I realized that is actually a crime since it's not mine, so I put it on your desk instead."

My eyes squinted open as I chuckled. "Why would you throw it away?"

The look she gave me said it all.

"Oh…"

"Yeah…"

I slid off the couch and wandered into the kitchen. I took my time puttering around…putting things away…making a snack…eating the snack…making small talk with Liza; basically, acting like I wasn't dying to read whatever he had written to me.

The sinking feeling in my heart and stomach were back full force, making me feel sick; yet somehow, I managed to stroll casually to my room.

Once I was behind my closed bedroom door, I immediately scooped up the letter and ripped it open.

Seeing his handwriting again caused all the progress I had made to come crashing down like a glacier plunging into the icy depths.

My dearest Scarlett,

I've been trying to call you for the past few months...and by "trying", I mean picking up the phone, dialing your number, and hanging up. I just couldn't think of anything that would explain my behavior on the last day I saw you...the day that I foolishly pushed you out of my life.

I keep replaying the things I said to you. The lies that I told to make you leave. I need you to know that I didn't mean a single word...and I cried my heart out when you ran out of my hospital room. The look on your face still kills me.

My parents told me that I was a fool to let you go, and they were right. I was just scared that you would wake up one day and realize that I was holding you back, and that I wasn't worth fighting for. I couldn't bear the thought of just being a stepping stone on your journey through life. So, I made the stupid decision to break your heart before you could break mine. I know now how silly and childish that was.

I guess what I'm trying to say is, that after everything we've been through, I want you to know that you were, and still are, the best thing that has ever happened to me. Your love was a gift that I never should have let go.

I've recently gotten my new prosthetic legs, so I am no longer stuck in my wheelchair. I have been working every day with my physical therapist. He really pushes me past my limit. A few weeks ago, I was actually able to walk the entire length of our foyer without stumbling at all, which I was told is a huge feat that should have been impossible so soon in the recovery process. *sigh* I'm rambling...I know...I just...I wanted to tell you how sorry I am for the things I said. And I hope that you can forgive me...and maybe one day we can be close again.

Yours Always, Alec

His words were blurred about halfway through, but I managed to make it to the end without completely losing my composure.

Shortly after that though, the tears overflowed.

CHAPTER 25

After receiving Alec's letter, I gave myself one week…one week to mull over my feelings, to see if they would change or fade. Neither happened. So, I called Lindy.

~*~*~*~

I pulled up to the Cavanaugh's gate, and my heart nearly pitter-pattered out of control. The thought of seeing Alec again after such a long time, especially given the circumstances in which we parted ways, had me on the verge of an anxiety attack. *You can face him,* I told myself. But doubt had already seeped into my thoughts.

I sat there for at least five minutes with my car idling, my mind spinning, and my palms sweating. When I finally gathered enough courage to reach for the keypad, a high-pitched ping, followed by a burst of static, emanated from the speaker.

I jumped involuntarily as an unfamiliar voice asked, "May I help you?"

Slightly caught off guard, I stuttered through my response. "Oh, um…I, well I'm…" I paused to clear my throat. "I'm here to see Al…I mean, uh Lindy. I'm here to see Lindy."

There was a moment of silence before the gates began to open. "Please drive around to the front, Miss Mitchel. Mrs. Cavanaugh will be waiting for you."

"Oh…okay," I said quietly. "Thank you."

I slowly drove through, watching the gates close in my rearview mirror. As I made my way up the long winding driveway, memories flashed in my mind from the last time I had been there. So many emotions seemed to be attacking me all at once.

My emotional state got even worse when the house finally came into view. A huge banner reading HAPPY BIRTHDAY CORA hung above the arch on the front porch. And at least a dozen other vehicles were all lined up along the side of the driveway. *Great. There went my plan for having a private moment with Alec.*

I parked behind the last vehicle, careful not to ruin the freshly cut grass, before making my way up the walkway. I hovered my hand over the doorbell, hesitating for only a second. But before I could press it, the double doors opened, and Lindy was standing on the other side.

"Ohh, Scarlett!" she gushed. "It is so good to see you!" Instantly she pulled me in for one of her famously big squeeze hugs. "How have you been?"

I laughed softly while returning her embrace. "I guess I've been alright. It's good to see you, too." *Please don't cry. Please don't cry.*

When we pulled apart, Lindy wiped her eyes and sighed with a faint smile forming. "It's been such a long and difficult road for him. Seeing you is exactly what he needs."

I forced a smile and asked, "Where is he? I'd like to talk to him before joining Cora's party."

Lindy nodded as she led me to the middle of the foyer. Suddenly, Sarge came racing around the corner, whining and yelping excitedly, his claws scraping against the marble floor. He nearly knocked me over as he skid to a stop against my feet.

I dropped to my knees and gave him a few overdo snuggles. "Aww, hey there sweet boy! I've missed you, too!"

Lindy chuckled as she pulled the large bundle of fur off me. "This big ol' beast has been enjoying his country life for the past eight months." She pat his head as his mouth hung open in a goofy expression. "I don't think he's going to want to go back to that little apartment."

I got up off the floor and grinned while giving Sarge's ears a good scratch, then he took off towards the sunroom and hopped up on one of the couches. "I don't blame him. I'd want to stay here, too." I paused and glanced her way. "So…how is Alec doing these days?"

Lindy sighed. "Well, he's been," she cleared her throat, "…he's doing much better. We had a rough start when we first brought him home. He couldn't really do anything on his own. So, we had to give him one of the guest rooms on the ground floor because he wasn't able to use the stairs. He refused any assistance from the in-home nurses. He wouldn't even allow them to touch him." She paused and ushered me into the study. "I don't think Alec would appreciate anyone else overhearing our conversation, so let's talk in here." She closed the door and sighed again before she continued, "Now I don't know if it was his stubbornness coming out, or if he was just so uncomfortable in his current state, but the fact remained that he was just so angry." She blew out her breath and shook her head. "He would cuss at the nurses all day long…throw things at them…he even threatened the last one, who happened to be a man, with bodily harm. It was evident very early on that Alec's confidence had been completely depleted. We finally realized that his father and I would have to become his primary caregivers. Not that he was too happy about that either, but it was better than having a stranger handling him. It was as if our twenty-seven-year-old son had reverted back into a baby. He couldn't bathe by himself; he couldn't go to the bathroom by himself; he couldn't even get out of bed by himself. After a few weeks, it was quite clear that he had fallen into a deep depression. There were so many nights that he would scream…all night long." Lindy paused again and stared at me with the most intense expression. "I'll be blunt with you, Scarlett. He called out your name quite often. I'm only telling you this so that you'll understand what he went through to get to where he is now. On those horrible nights when Alec's cries would wake his father and me from a dead sleep, we would come rushing in to check on him, but he always threw us out. We honestly thought we were going to lose him." She sighed again as a soft laugh escaped. "Then one day, he just woke up with the most determined attitude I had ever seen. He refused to listen to the doctors anymore. All of their negative comments were doing nothing but bringing him down…bringing all of us down actually. Every day after that, the dark cloud that had been plaguing our family seemed to have been lifted. Alec was laughing again; he was smiling again; he was enjoying life again. And I'll never forget the day that he took his first steps on his prosthetics. He was so damn proud! He only managed to take three small strides before he fell, but the happiness on his face never faltered. I felt like I was witnessing his first steps as a toddler all over again." She paused to wipe her eyes. "Oh, listen to me babbling on and on when you should be upstairs hearing all this from him."

I reached out to hug her. "No, it's okay. I'm glad you told me. Thank you."

Lindy returned my embrace and gave me a quick kiss on the cheek. "Alright now," she stated while regaining her composure. "Everyone is still out by the lake getting ready to have some barbecue," she paused and grinned, "Henry is in his element with that oversized grill…but Alec had gone upstairs to change about fifteen minutes ago. So, I'm sure he's decent by now. You can head on up. Do you remember where his room is?"

"Yeah," I whispered. "I remember."

Lindy sighed deeply and gave my hand a squeeze as she opened the door. "Before you go, you should know that I didn't tell him you were coming..." She eyed me sadly. "...just in case you changed your mind. I didn't want to get his hopes up."

I swallowed nervously as my stomach did an uneasy flip. "Oh..."

"Don't worry, dear." Lindy smiled warmly. "He will be thrilled to see you."

I smiled back, though I was not one-hundred percent sure of that statement. "I hope so," I replied timidly.

"He will be," she reassured me. "I can promise you that." She hugged me once again before she walked away.

I caught sight of Henry in the next room. Lindy touched his shoulder and whispered something, which caused him to glance my way. He smiled in my direction and offered up a little wave, which I respectfully returned, before heading toward the stairs as quickly as possible.

I paused on the bottom step, gripping the railing for dear life.

Bikini-clad bodies were muddling about everywhere while music was blaring from the stereo in the sunroom. Squeals and laughter echoed all around me while Cora and her friends were laughing and dancing without a care in the world.

I made a silent wish for that happiness to fill me and take away the nervousness that was currently engulfing my body.

When I made it to the second floor, I paused again on the landing, trying to gather some courage. Then I made my way down the hall and stood outside Alec's bedroom door. I blew out my breath in a quick burst before raising my fist.

Three gentle knocks later, I heard Alec say, "It's open," from the other side.

I reached for the handle and instantly lost my nerve.

"It's open!" Alec repeated a bit louder.

I swallowed down my doubt and gave the door a little shove.

Alec's back was facing my direction, and he was currently standing in a pair of blue and white board shorts, just about to slip a tank top over his head. His dark hair was longer than when I had seen him last, and still damp, a tell-tale sign that he had recently been in the lake.

I immediately noticed that his beautiful body was much more muscular than I remembered. Must have been from all the physical therapy he had been doing.

As my eyes took him in for the first time in months, his new prosthetic legs caught my eye in the most amazing way possible. Each one had been painted to match the tattoo on his arm. The right leg was the hellfire, except that the outstretched hand was missing, and the flames seemed to be being doused with water. The left leg was a near-perfect duplication of the full galaxy, with one significant detail change. There were a pair of hands in a praying position with the words 'strength', 'faith', and 'overcome' written around it in a perfect circle.

I smiled involuntarily as I thought about the undeniable strength that this man had within. Even if he did throw away everything we had between us, he still managed to overcome seemingly impossible odds.

Not even a minute later, Alec turned around, finally realizing that someone was standing in his room. His eyes widened in surprise as he finished tugging his tank top into place. He reached out to hug me, probably out of habit, but at the last second, he awkwardly pulled his arms back.

Eight long months had passed since we had last been face to face. Both of us stood there staring at each other, not saying anything. But then Alec broke the silence first with just a single word.

"Hi," he said quietly.

My heart instantly skipped a beat. "Hi," I returned.

"You got my letter?"

I nodded in response.

He let out a tortured sigh. "I'm so sorry, Scarlett," he whispered.

He continued staring at me until I just could not take it anymore, so I briefly looked away.

"I hate that I hurt you," his voice cracked. "And even worse, I hate that I lied to you. I never should have…but I just…I was completely destroyed after the accident, in every sense of the word. Losing my legs left me in a very dark place, full of despair and self-hatred. The inside of me seemed to match the outside for a long time; disfigured and missing pieces…"

"But I never saw you that way," I finally managed to choke out. "You were never broken…you were never disfigured. You were just…you." I paused to take a breath. "I told you, time and time again, that I wanted to be there for you! To be by your side through all the hurdles of your recovery…instead, you pushed me away in the most insensitive and uncaring manner. And then after months and months of agonizing silence, when I finally managed to regain some sense of my life, you decided to write me a letter, telling me that you didn't mean any of the horrible things you said to me! I just don't understand you at all! It's like you're two people in one, and I never know who I'm going to come face to face with…happy and loving Alec, or angry and aggressive Alec."

He took a small step toward me. "I'm so sorry," he sobbed. "I know how badly I screwed things up between us, and I hate the way I handled everything! I'm not trying to make excuses here, but I've never been able to express myself well. You know that. I just lash out in any way that I can to keep from ever getting hurt."

"But why do you keep lashing out at *me*? I feel like you are completely unpredictable…and that I have to walk on eggshells just to keep you happy! You really do scare me when you're angry, Alec! I never know what you're capable of!"

He sighed painfully as he took another step closer. "I would never hurt you intentionally, Scarlett. You have to know that much! And I swear that I will try harder to make sure you never have to walk on eggshells for me ever again."

"I want to believe you," I whispered. "…but I don't know how I…"

"I just need one more chance," he pleaded. "One more chance to prove that I can be the man you deserve." He was silent for a few seconds before his breath exhaled in a shudder. "In the process of losing myself, I lost the only person I really wanted to be with through all this…through everything. Scarlett, I…I love you with every fiber of my existence…and I just wish I would have told you that sooner…before I…" His words trailed off.

I had planned to hold it together…to keep my wits about myself…to hold my ground…but seeing him face to face, smelling his cologne, hearing his voice, and listening to him beg for my forgiveness while declaring his love for me, was much harder than I could have ever expected. So, when the tears came, they exploded from my body in a desperate and powerful rush.

Alec immediately stepped forward without any hesitation and wrapped his arms around me, pulling me hard against his chest. Out of nowhere, his tears came full force, and soon, neither of us could breathe. "I despise myself for scaring you…" he whimpered. "…and for making you doubt my true intentions."

The last of my composure crumbled. All the love and passion that I had locked away, inadvertently came flooding back. "I don't even know who you are anymore, Alec."

His grip tightened around me. "I didn't either…" he choked out. "Not for a long time. My state of mind that day was completely unstable! The pain I was in…it wasn't just physical, but I...I didn't understand what I was feeling. The entire situation was affecting my mental and emotional states." He paused to take in a few shallow breaths. "I knew what I was saying to you. I understood the words that were leaving my mouth, but I didn't think ahead about the consequences that would follow. I was just so angry. Angry for how I handled the situation with you and Brock...angry at you for not listening to me and hearing me out...angry at my parents for not talking me out of coming to see you...angry at myself for foolishly ignoring the signs on that damn curvy road...angry at God for not healing my injuries...angry at the doctors for taking my legs..." He paused again and sighed painfully. "It was just too much, and I felt completely overwhelmed and entirely unprepared for what was happening to me..."

I tried to stifle another violent sob.

Alec did, too. "I did figure out one crucial thing during all this," he added.

"What's that?" I whimpered.

"That I'm nothing without you."

A loud wail escaped my mouth as more tears made their way down my cheeks. I was unable to stop them by that point.

"I know you're nowhere near ready to forgive me..." he whispered dismally. "But one day...I pray that you will be able to."

My lips quivered as I struggled to regain some of my composure, but that was proving rather difficult. "I forgave you a long time ago, Alec..."

A tortured sigh left his lips. "You have no idea how much that means to me!" Alec's words got harder and harder to understand as he struggled to calm himself down. "I was told that I'd never walk again," he cried out. "That most people with a double amputation are wheelchair bound, dependent on their loved ones for the rest of their lives. I struggled daily with that thought circling around in my mind. I thought about how hard it would be for my family to have to take care of me every second of every damn day. My parents would have to help me get dressed and help me bathe as if I was an infant. They would have to use a special vehicle to take me everywhere because I wouldn't be able to drive…not to mention, having to install a ramp so I could get in and out of the house!" He paused again and shook his head sadly. "So many changes were taking place in my life...changes that I didn't want and didn't ask for…and I just…I wasn't willing to accept any of it. Some rather dark thoughts crossed my mind. Thoughts that I'm too ashamed to speak out loud. When I imagined myself stuck in that chair for the rest of my life…I muddled over the thought of just giving up; but in the end, I had to prove them all wrong. I had to stand on my own. I had to walk. I had to dance again. And you…you helped with all that."

I stumbled through my reply. "How…how could I have possibly helped you? I…I wasn't even there!"

"But you were," he replied quickly. He placed his hand over his heart as a muffled sob escaped his lips. "You were always with me. Through every painful step…through every distressing fall…through every frustrating setback. You were my guiding force, pushing me forward when I wanted nothing more than to throw in the towel."

A powerful moan escaped my mouth before I collapsed to the floor. My legs had actually given out on me, and my body began folding in on itself.

A split second later, I heard the sound of the bedroom door opening, but I couldn't see through my blurry vision who was standing there.

Alec quickly shouted, "GET OUT," and immediately, whoever it was backed away, and I heard a soft click as the door closed again.

Alec managed to maneuver himself to where he could sit down beside me on the floor. He gently pulled me into his lap and brushed my hair away from my face. "I didn't want to be a burden to you." His whispered voice cracked when he spoke. "And at that point, that's all I was."

"You would have never been..." I couldn't even finish my sentence.

Alec hugged me closer. "I know that now. But after so much time had gone by, I didn't think you could ever forgive me...especially when I couldn't even forgive myself. I'm broken, Scarlett. In every sense of the word. And this..." He touched his prosthetics. "It was just another flaw."

"Stop saying that!" I practically shouted the words as I lifted myself up so I could look him in the eyes. "Why do you keep repeating such horrible things about yourself? You're beautiful, Alec! I've told you that time and time again!"

He cupped my face in his hands and let out a shaky breath. "*You* are everything beautiful in my life. Everything wonderful. Everything good. Everything I never thought I deserved...but I'm..." He nearly choked on his own words. "I'm never going to be worthy of you. You deserve so much more than I could ever give you."

"That's not true!" I argued.

"Up until I met you, women felt sorry for me...or they would just use me once they realized that I had money...such a cliché thing really...that was all I ever knew. Now...when people see me, they have stares of pity and sympathy, nothing more..."

My eyes widened as I interrupted him. "And you thought that I would be like that? That I'm just some shallow, superficial bitch that's going to..."

He immediately cut me off. "No!"

I struggled to breathe as tears continued to stream down my face. "Clearly you did...or you wouldn't have said those things...and you wouldn't have pushed me away! You wouldn't have left me..."

"Scarlett, look at yourself!" he stated angrily. "And look at me!" His unsteady breathing became more and more erratic as he fumbled a bit with trembling hands as he took off his prosthetics, revealing his fully healed appendages.

"I *am* looking at you!" I countered.

The two of us sat there staring at each other for quite some time, just sniffling, not saying a word.

I glanced down at the thick scar tissue covering what was left of his knees. Then without any warning, I knelt on the floor in front of him, my tears falling against his skin.

Before he had a chance to react, I leaned over to kiss the scars on both of his legs. When I glanced up, his facial expression was the most tortured thing that I had ever seen.

"Scarlett…" he breathed shakily.

I sighed deeply and wiped my eyes. "It's not true, ya know?"

"What?" he asked breathlessly.

"Any of it." I raised up, bracing my hands on either side of his thighs until we were tear-ridden face to tear-ridden face. "You drive me completely insane, and some days I just wanna strangle-hug you until all the negativity toward yourself falls away! Then you would see what I see. That you are amazing…and handsome…and beautiful…and worthy of everything good…of everything you've ever dreamed of."

He sighed painfully. "You're only saying those things because you care about me…because we're…friends again?"

A laugh escaped my lips as I shook my head, sniffling once more. "You really are daft sometimes."

He stared back at me with sad eyes.

I caressed his face, wiping away a stray tear from his cheek. "I don't just care about you as a friend, Alec. And I sure as hell don't make love to my friends. How can you not see that after everything we've gone through?"

His eyes were wide open at that point, and he was currently holding his breath. "After all I put you though, I just assumed…"

"You assumed wrong." A soft laugh escaped me again. "I

love you, too, ya dummy."

Tiny streams were flowing down his face. "Really? Even with...?" He glanced down at his legs without finishing his question.

I gently stroked his face, tilting his chin so that he had to look at me again. "Even with..."

A soft chuckle escaped his tear-stained lips. "I love you, Scarlett...more than you can ever imagine."

CHAPTER 26

Hand in hand, Alec and I made our way downstairs to join in the rest of Cora's birthday celebration.

Through the windows of the sunroom, I could see that the entire boardwalk was lit up with paper lanterns of all different colors and sizes, each one connected to the other to form a canopy that illuminated the area in a rainbow effect.

Beyond that, a two-story party barge was floating in the middle of the lake, complete with a slide attached at the back. Jet skis raced through the water, causing little waves in their wake.

Multicolored floatable devices were everywhere, and people were splashing and screaming with laughter while music blared from an oversized karaoke system set up on the dock. The current pick was 'Can't Stop This Thing We Started' by Bryan Adams.

As the chorus began, Alec lifted my hand above my head and twirled me around before leading me outside.

A large table full of delicious food greeted us. Hotdogs, hamburgers, shrimp, chicken, steak, fries, chips, fruit, veggies, condiments, brownies, cupcakes, all types of candy…you name it, they had it.

Henry was standing in front of a grill a few feet away. He turned around and offered us a friendly wave as he swayed from side to side to the beat of the music while flipping some more burgers.

Just beyond him, a group of people were playing volleyball. The outline of the player's section was lined with bright red tiki torches, and the net was wrapped in blue fairy-lights, giving the surrounding area an ethereal glow.

My wide eyes gazed up at Alec. "Shesh, you guys really go all out for parties, eh?"

He grinned. "Not a penny was spared in the quest to make Princess Cora happy."

"I heard that!" Cora chirped. She held up her red plastic cup and continued to dance with her friends.

Alec chuckled and turned to me. "Can I get you a drink?"

I smiled. "Sure."

"Alcoholic or non?"

I gave him *the look*.

He laughed. "Got it."

As Alec walked away, I strolled over to where his dad was still cooking, to see if I could help in any way. "Hey, Henry. How's it goin'?"

"Oh, hey there, Scarlett! It's good to see you, dear."

I giggled. "It's good to see you, too."

Henry smiled. "I'm just chillin' and grillin' like a villain."

Lindy appeared behind us, laughing. She handed me a soda. "Alec asked me to give you this." Then she put her hand lovingly on her husband's shoulder. "I think it might be time to lay off the scotch, my love."

Henry held up his spatula and looked at his wife with the most serious expression. "So, it's probably too late to confess that I spiked the punch earlier?"

Lindy's mouth dropped open. "Henry William

Cavanaugh! There will be hell to pay if you really…"

Henry's growing grin stopped her mid-sentence.

Suddenly, reverb and a high-pitched ping caused me, Lindy, and Henry to cover our ears. We glanced around; everyone else was doing the same thing.

"My apologies," Alec's voice echoed. He tapped the microphone on the stand in front of him. "I know this night is all about my wonderful sister and her existence on this planet…" Alec paused and pointed at Cora. "I love you, big sis, I truly do, and I wish you a Happy Birthday!"

Cora yelled out, "I love you, little bro! Wooooooo!"

Alec chuckled into the microphone. "With that being said, I'd like to take a moment to acknowledge my beautiful girlfriend, Scarlett."

I blushed and temporarily covered my smiling face.

"As most of you already know, I had a very difficult time coming back after my accident. In turn, I ended up pushing away the most important person in my life. It's something I've been struggling with, and was too ashamed to talk about. But today…" He paused as his blue eyes locked onto mine. "Today she decided to give me a second chance." He flashed me his perfect smile. "No words could ever express how thankful I am to have you back…but I hope this song is a start."

He leaned over and typed something on the karaoke machine; then he cleared his throat as he clipped the microphone back onto the stand.

A gentle piano melody filtered through the speakers just before Alec's angelic voice began to croon 'Everything I Do, I Do It For You' by Bryan Adams.

I felt as if I was watching a music video on VH1…with the sun disappearing behind the mountains in the distance…him belting out each note with flawless accuracy…and his smoldering gaze solely fixated on me.

The passion and love coming from his words were being poured into my soul, etching his name forever on my heart.

As the song slowly came to an end, applause erupted from all the guests.

Tears welled in my eyes as I stared at the beautiful man in front of me that was destined to be my soulmate.

As the last musical notes faded away, Alec sighed deeply, keeping his stare on me.

I mouthed the words, *I love you.*

To which, he smiled and instantly walked over to scoop me up in his arms. "I love you, too," he whispered in my ear. "Always and forever."

For the rest of the evening, the focus was back on the birthday girl. We played volleyball; went swimming; enjoyed a few laps on a jet ski; and then everyone gathered together to have dinner under the stars.

The night ended with a bang…and a bunch of sparkles…as a vibrantly elaborate show of fireworks exploded overhead.

Standing in the glow of the moon, watching Alec's face being lit up by all the beautiful lights, was like my own personal glimpse of heaven. And boy, did I love the view.

CHAPTER 27

Alec and I spent nearly every day together after that.

We even danced at the 1999 Halloween Ball, on the same dance floor, in the same spot where we had first met face to face the year before. But that time, I was able to join in with the 'Thriller' dance because I had a fantastic teacher helping me to learn the steps.

Thanksgiving was spent at my family's cabin, while Christmas was at the Cavanaugh's mansion.

Henry and my dad had become the best of friends; the same could be said for my mom and Lindy. Even Cora had fully warmed up to me. I went out with her and Liza at least once every weekend for a girls' night. It was as if the universe was giving us every sign that we were meant to be.

~*~*~*~

With New Year's Day quickly approaching, everyone we knew was a mixture of excited and nervous. Rumors had been spreading like wildfire that when the clock struck midnight, and the date on our computers changed from the year 1999 to 2000, the entire internet superhighway would completely shut down because the data for all the zeros would be invalid.

People all over the world were calling it Y2K, or the Year 2000 Problem. It was like the countdown to the Internet Apocalypse.

Alec and I decided to invite everyone we knew to a New Year's party to try and ease their worry and stress. Much to our surprise, every single person we invited accepted our invitation. Which meant that we had to have the party at his parents' mansion, because it was the biggest piece of property to hold such a large gathering.

When my parents and I arrived just before nightfall, the entire curving driveway was teeming with vehicles, bumper to bumper, all the way back to the gate. Of course, Alec had told me that we could park inside one of the garage bays, so we didn't have to walk very far.

As the double doors to the house opened, there were multicolored streamers and white fairy-lights everywhere…hanging from the ceiling, wrapping around all the railings and columns, and separating rooms as if they were flowing doorways.

Funny glasses, hats, and strobe-light jewelry all sporting the year 2000 were lying on a table in the foyer for guests to pick up and put on as they entered.

No sooner had I walked in the door, Alec's smiling face greeted me and I was pulled in for a hug. With one arm still wrapped around me, he extended his hand toward my dad. "It's nice to see you again, Joseph. I hope things at work haven't been too stressful."

My dad chuckled and returned the handshake. "Just the usual. Too many bad guys, too little time to catch them all. But it is good to see you. Where has your father run off to?"

Alec laughed. "He's outside, probably checking on the fireworks display for the hundredth time."

"I'll go give him a hand then," my dad replied with a smile.

Then Alec turned toward my mom, only releasing me to give her a welcoming hug. "And how are you doing, Mae? I heard you went out with my mother and my aunts last weekend."

My mom stood on her tip-toes to give him a quick kiss on the cheek. "Oh, yes. It was quite a lovely outing. Your family is just so wonderful. We think the world of you all."

Alec laughed softly. "We think the world of you, too."

My mom slowly released her hold on him. "I'd like to have some time to speak with your mother before we go outside. Is she busy?"

Alec took a step back and gestured toward the kitchen. "She's probably making more food, even after hiring three of the best caterers in the Carolinas."

My mom smiled. "I'll go drag her away…and maybe sneak a sample or two before everyone else gets some."

Alec laughed out loud. "Good luck with that. Most of my old college buddies showed up early and have been trying to get past security…a-k-a, my sister."

My mom's laughter echoed as she walked away. "I'll make it past Princess Cora."

Alec shook his head smiling as he sweetly entwined our fingers and kissed the back of my hand. "Come with me. There are some people I want you to meet."

Out on the back deck, a large crowd of our nearest and dearest friends were dancing and tossing huge balloons into the air, all wearing a mixture of the year 2000 accessories.

Alec and I weaved our way through the mass of bodies until we were close to the end of the dock. There, I immediately recognized Brock amongst a small group of guys, along with two girls, which caused a sinking feeling to settle in my gut.

On our approach, all of them turned and started calling out Alec's name, welcoming him with slaps on the back and high fives. The two girls practically jumped into his arms, nearly spilling their drinks.

That image was exactly what I had imagined when I thought about his playboy partying past...constantly surrounded by beautiful women and booze...but instead of giving in to my fight-or-flight response that was so desperately trying to kick in, I decided to give Alec the benefit of the doubt and see how he was going to handle the situation.

Alec gave each of them a hug, as I expected he would, before hastily removing himself from their grasp. He took a step back and held his hand out behind him, waiting for me to take it. When I did, he gently tugged me forward until we were side by side.

"Vanessa...Sabrina...this is Scarlett."

Hearing their names sent my mind back to the day when we first fell apart, causing me to accidentally grip Alec's hand a bit tighter.

He glanced down at me and smiled, completely oblivious to my current state of mind. "These are some of my friends from college. Vanessa, Sebrina, Donovan, Kevin, Randy, Declan, and Mike. You already know Brock."

Hands were thrust in my direction for welcoming handshakes.

Vanessa was the last one to step closer to Alec. "So, this is the woman who stole your heart? It's about time you introduced her to us!" She turned toward me and smiled. "We've heard of nothing else for so long that I feel like I already know you!"

Instead of shaking my hand like everyone else had, she pulled me in for a rather unexpected hug.

I let out a nervous chuckle while returning her embrace.

After that, all the negative feelings that had been bottled up inside of me seemed to melt away. I was actually able to let loose and enjoy myself.

Nearly all of my co-workers, my boss included, showed up to celebrate. So, it was turning out to be quite a wonderful night.

Close to 10:00pm, Alec got on a microphone and asked everyone to head over to the volleyball area.

As I made my way over, I noticed a huge white screen with a projector nearby, surrounded by enough cushions and blankets to appease every single guest.

Alec waited until everyone had gathered around the screen before he continued, "The countdown to the new year has begun, so while we wait, I'd like everyone to make themselves comfortable on one of the many pallets spread out across the lawn. There are coolers full of snacks and drinks beside each one, so we can relax and watch a movie. Not only is it a classic, but also a film very close to my heart."

He paused as multiple people blurted out, "What movie?"

"The Princess Bride," he replied quickly.

Without waiting for any other responses, Alec clipped the microphone back onto the stand and searched the crowd until his eyes landed on me. Then he walked toward me with his perfect smile spreading across his gorgeous face.

I crossed my arms and grinned. "Nice choice for a film."

He pulled me in for another hug. "As you wish," he whispered.

I sighed against his chest as I wrapped my arms around him. "As you wish, indeed."

We settled into a pallet closest to the screen so that Alec could control the projector. Then we snuggled together while playfully tossing candy at each other.

~*~*~*~

Nearing the end of the movie, Alec leaned over and whispered in my ear, "It's nearly midnight…"

I glanced in his direction. "Almost time for fireworks then," I whispered back.

He grinned and licked his lips as his Adam's-apple bobbed in his throat. "Yeah, but…will you come with me for a second…before all that starts? I just need to talk to you about something in private."

My stomach did that familiar uneasy flip. "Is everything okay?"

He nodded. "I just want to talk to you before the new year."

I sat up straighter. "You're kinda worrying me with your tone," I whispered. A nervous laugh followed.

Alec abruptly stood and offered me his hand. "Just come with me. Please."

No one else seemed to be paying us any mind as we stepped around and over people as we headed toward the house.

Alec led me up the stairs and gestured toward his bedroom door. "There's something special in there for you, so I'd like you to go first if you don't mind."

I eyed him suspiciously. "What are you up to, Mr. Phantom?"

He casually crossed his arms across his chest and leaned against the wall. "My smiling lips are zipped."

I chuckled and shook my head. "Okay, fine. I'll bite." Then I grabbed the handle and opened the door.

"Let me get the light switch," Alec told me as he reached around my shoulder.

My breath escaped in an awe-struck rush as the darkness in front of me instantly disappeared. A bright light illuminated the room, revealing a multitude of multicolored bouquets. Roses, orchids, and sunflowers were everywhere I looked. When I glanced down, countless red, white, and pink rose petals were scattered all over the floor by my feet.

I stepped inside, smiling, as I inhaled the sweet floral scent. The trail of delicate petals led straight to Alec's king-sized bed, where I could see even more of them spread across his cream-colored duvet. As I got closer, I noticed that each velvety petal was carefully placed to spell out four specific words.

I spun around in complete surprise.

Alec walked over to stand beside his bed. That was when he reached into his pocket and took out a small black box. As he lifted the lid, my eyes landed on a beautiful diamond and sapphire ring.

My hand reflexively covered my mouth, which had fallen open from shock.

His eyes were glistening as his trembling lips began to smile. "I would kneel, but…"

I must have stood there for a full minute before I was able to move. Then a soft laugh escaped me as I rushed forward, leaping into his arms, causing both of us to topple backward onto the bed.

Soft, sweet-smelling rose petals surrounded us as our blissful laughter echoed throughout the room.

Alec tucked my hair behind my ear as he leaned up to kiss the tip of my nose. "Soooo…is that a yes?"

I bit my bottom lip as tears welled in my eyes. "Yes…a million times, yes!"

"Oh, thank God!" Alec blew out his breath and went completely limp as if he was sighing with relief.

I giggled and shoved his chest. "Psht, like there was ever any doubt what my answer would be."

A grin tugged at the corner of his mouth as he brought my hand closer. "I'm just so thankful that I will get to spend forever with you." He spoke those precious words as he slipped the ring onto my finger.

I held out my hand to inspect my sparkling accessory. "It's perfect."

"Yes, you are," Alec replied.

"I know you are," I whispered.

Alec smiled while caressing my cheek. "As you wish, my Buttercup."

I hovered my face above his. "I love you, too, my Westley."

Then he pulled me closer for a passionate, gentle kiss.

~*~*~*~

When we went back downstairs, everyone had gathered at the bottom landing, staring at us intensely as if they had been waiting for us the whole time.

Alec reached for my hand and turned it over so that my oversized diamond was glittering in the light, then he shouted, "SHE SAID YES!"

Ear-piercing screams and applause filled the room, followed by, "Congratulations!" as everyone joined together to celebrate our brand-new engagement.

"TO ALEC AND SCARLETT!" they all cheered.

As most of the guests made their way back outside chatting excitedly, I watched as my mom and Liza shoved their way through the crowd. When they got to the base of the stairs, I practically tackle hugged them while squealing with excitement.

"Oh, honey!" my mom gushed. "We are so happy for you two!" Then she grabbed Alec. "Welcome to the family, sweetheart!"

"And to think...Alec put all this together in just a few weeks," Liza added.

I looked back and forth between the three of them. "Huh?"

My mom pulled me back in for another hug. "Your handsome fiancé came to your father and me just after Thanksgiving and asked us for your hand..."

I glanced up at Alec, tears glistening. "You did?" My voice came out as a little squeak.

He smiled as he came down another step. "I wanted to do things right. I wanted everything to be perfect for you."

"It was...it is...everything is perfect." I paused to take a breath.

A few minutes later, after the majority of the guests had gone back outside, my dad, and Alec's parents joined in with the jumping, squealing group hug.

Cora came running up calling our names. "C'mon you

lovebirds! It's time!"

No sooner had we walked back out onto the deck, everyone began to shout in unison, "10... 9... 8... 7... 6... 5... 4... 3... 2... 1... HAPPY NEW YEAR!"

The confetti cannons and the fireworks went off a split second later, lighting up the sky in a rainbow of sparkles and glitter.

The rest of the evening, Alec and I enjoyed our time being surrounded by all those we held dear…and we were congratulated so many times that I lost count.

Around 3:00am, when the party started to die down, and the majority of our guests had either gone home or passed out, Cora announced, "Should we turn on the computer to see if technology as we know it has come to an end?"

There were close to fifty of us, all gathered in the library, surrounding the desk. Alec turned on the computer and waited to see if it would boot up.

So far, so good.

He clicked on the AOL icon and the dialing commenced. The usual pings of static and the high-pitched screeching sounds filtered through the speakers.

At that point, everyone leaned in closer, practically holding their breath as the connecting icon popped up. Then the familiar sound of "You've Got Mail!" echoed throughout the room, followed by a few *whoops* and *hoots* and sighs of relief.

We were all happy to find that the internet, and all its ones and zeros, had in fact survived the journey into the new year.

~*~*~*~

A month later, Alec and I sent out invitations to our wedding.

CHAPTER 28

~*~*~*~*~*~*~*~*~*~*~*~*~*~*~*~

Join us in celebrating the union between

Alec Xavier Cavanaugh

and

Scarlett Elena Mitchel

On the eve of March 17th, 2000.

~*~*~*~*~*~*~*~*~*~*~*~*~*~*~*~

Exactly two years after we had met online, we said, "I do" in front of all our family and friends in a quaint little church in the countryside.

At the reception, Alec stood beside me at our table and raised his champagne glass toward the crowd. "I want to thank you all for coming, and for sharing in our special day. Scarlett and I are so blessed to be surrounded by so many wonderful people." Then he turned to me. "Two years ago to the day, I met this woman...this extraordinary woman...who

I now have the privilege to call my wife." He paused and smiled. "I don't know what I did to deserve a gift like you, Scarlett, but I thank God every single day for bringing you into my life and for showing me the meaning of true love."

He leaned down and kissed my cheek, then whispered in my ear. "You are forever my favorite 'scar'."

I smiled as tears filled my eyes. "I love you," I whispered.

"I love you, more."

I grabbed Alec's arm and pulled him into my lap in front of everyone; then I kissed him with every ounce of passion flowing within me.

His strong hands caressed my face as cheers erupted throughout the room, encasing us in an invisible bubble of love, acceptance, and a newly acquired appreciation for the life we had been given.

CHAPTER 29

One year later...

I paced back in forth in the kitchen while impatiently waiting for Alec to get home from work. I glanced at the clock again. He should be arriving within the next ten to fifteen minutes.

Sarge's claws clickety-clacked on the floor as he followed my every move.

I stopped pacing to give him a gentle pat on the head. "I'm okay, boy." *Okay, my ass!* My mind scolded me. Then a few seconds later, my stomach tightened.

I glanced down at the little plastic stick in my hand. A vibrant pink plus-sign was staring back at me, refusing to be ignored. "Oh, God," I muttered out loud. *How could this have happened?* I thought helplessly. Alec and I had been so careful. I was always on time with taking my birth control, and on top of that, Alec always insisted on wearing a condom as an added precaution.

I had noticed some changes in my body over the past few weeks, but the possibility of being pregnant never actually crossed my mind. Even when I was late, I just told myself that it was because of stress. But it had been almost two months since I experienced my 'monthly friend'.

So, that morning, I waited until Alec had gone to work and then I raced to the nearest store to buy a pregnancy test.

The box said to wait at least three minutes for any lines to appear, but no sooner had I put the little cap back on, a plus sign was already as bright as could be.

I threw up a moment later. The shock, combined with my apparent pregnancy hormones, was just too much.

My mind kept going back to the night where Alec and I had discussed how he felt about having a biological child of his own…the worry and dread that engulfed him every time he thought about the possibility of passing on the Treacher Collins gene. And now, I had to tell him that his worst fear may actually become a reality.

I placed my hand on my stomach just as I heard the front door open.

"Babe! I'm home!" Alec called out.

Please don't throw up again, I told myself.

Sarge had run off to greet his master, so I sat down at the table, struggling to find the words to deliver the news as gently as possible.

The moment Alec and Sarge appeared in the archway, I had to make a bee-line straight for the garbage can.

Great. I really hope this isn't an omen of what my entire pregnancy is going to be like.

Alec was by my side in a flash, holding my hair out of the way and rubbing my back. "Sweetheart, are you alright?"

I groaned as another wave of nausea overtook me. Even the thought of opening my mouth to tell him the news caused me to dry heave again and again.

Alec grabbed a glass from the nearest cabinet and filled it with water; then he went looking for the bottle of Tums. "Should I call the doctor and make you an appointment? Maybe you caught the flu. It has been going around."

I shook my head as my stomach finally began to settle. "No. I'm fine. But there is something I need to tell you."

I chewed the Tums slowly and then gulped down a few swigs of water.

When I turned around to face him, Alec had his back to me, and he was looking down at something in his hands.

Oh no! I had dropped the test in my rush to get to the garbage can.

When Alec turned around, his eyes were wide, his forehead was creased, and his mouth was hanging open. "Scarlett...?"

I instinctively reached for my stomach again. "I just found out this morning."

Alec let out a shuddered breath as he collapsed onto one of our dining chairs. "But we were so careful," he whispered. His gaze eventually shifted towards me. "I didn't even know you were late."

"My cycle was never regular, so I didn't think I had anything to worry about."

"How long ago...?"

"Two months...maybe."

Alec placed the test on the table and looked away as he began to rub his temples. "We're going to have a baby." His voice was barely audible, so I wasn't sure of his tone.

"Yeah. We are," I replied quietly as that old nervous lump lodged itself in my throat.

"We're going to have a baby," he repeated slightly louder. Then he looked back up at me. He was smiling with tears in his eyes. "Oh, Scarlett!" Alec suddenly pulled me into his lap, wrapping his arms around me. He placed his hand on my belly with such a delicate touch, as if he was afraid he might break something.

I placed my hand on top of his. "So...you're not upset?"

"My beautiful wife is pregnant with my first-born child." Alec let out a soft laugh as his other hand caressed my face. "I am feeling so many emotions right now, but upset is not one of them."

"But I thought...?"

"I know," he sighed, interrupting. "So did I. But this…"
He paused and laughed again while rubbing my stomach.
"…this is a miracle. Our little miracle."

"But the possibility of passing on the gene…" I paused
and sighed. "That could still happen."

Alec sighed, too. "I know. And I will probably feel an
extreme amount of sadness and guilt if our baby does end up
having TCS, but at the same time, I will be so damn proud to
be his or her father…and I will love them, and their amazing
mother, until my very last breath."

I bit my lip to hide my growing smile as tears of relief
made their way down my cheeks.

CHAPTER 30

The very next morning, I called my obstetrician. I explained the situation and how worried I was. She told me to come in that afternoon for the earliest appointment available, which was at 2:30pm.

After sitting for what seemed like an eternity in the overcrowded waiting room, it turned out that I was only six weeks along…too early to know anything. But we were told that the fetus was healthy and seemed to be growing as expected.

That evening, Alec and I sat in our living room, brainstorming for the perfect way to tell our parents that we were expecting a little bundle of joy.

Alec turned to me, grinning from ear to ear. "I've got a great idea!"

~*~*~*~

Three days later, our custom-made surprise arrived in the mail. I opened the package and felt tears prick my eyes. "This is going to be perfect," I said to myself.

Alec came around the corner. "Are all the pieces there?"

I closed the box and nodded. "I can't wait to see their faces!"

He kissed the top of my head. "They're going to love it. There will be tears of joy for sure."

I wrapped my arms around his neck. "It's been so hard to keep this a secret, especially given that I talk to my parents on a daily basis."

He sighed. "I know. But this weekend we will invite them all over and have a big celebration."

I gave him a little squeeze. "I can't wait!"

~*~*~*~

Late Saturday afternoon, I poured out the box, letting the puzzle pieces tumble onto the table. I made sure to turn each one over so that the colored sides would be on top. Then, I set a picture frame in the center of the table, placing the first puzzle piece in the top corner to start the process.

Alec and I sat anxiously in our living room, waiting for our parents to arrive for dinner.

His mom and dad showed up first. Of course, they brought their best bottle of wine. A short while later, my parents knocked on the door.

We started off the evening by having everyone help with setting the table.

Dinnertime was full of old stories and lots of laughs. Everyone was chatting and enjoying the delicious meal. After dessert, we all retired to the den to enjoy some wine.

It wasn't until Lindy inquired why I hadn't touched my glass, that I changed the subject and asked them all to join us in the guest room.

The confused expressions on their faces made me and Alec chuckle.

We ushered the four of them into the room. "Alright, so I've divided up the puzzle pieces so that each of you have an equal amount. All you have to do is work together to put the pieces in the right places."

After a few more glasses of wine, and some playful bickering, our parents had managed to finish their task.

The end result was a picture of me, Alec, and Sarge that

had been taken for last year's Christmas cards.

The questioning stares meant that it was time to reveal the surprise.

I slid the back panel onto the frame, covering our picture.

Another round of silent, yet perplexed expressions from each of our parents.

"What are you two up to?" my dad finally asked.

Alec came to stand beside me.

"We thought you all would want to know..." Instead of finishing my sentence, I turned the picture frame around and sat it in front of them.

Written on the other side, was a special message: *We don't know if it's a HE or a SHE...but what we'd like you to know, is that you are grandparents to be!*

"OH, MY GOD!"

"WE'RE GOING TO BE GRANDPARENTS?"

"Is this real? Are you really...?"

"I'm gonna be a grandma?"

"I'M GOING TO BE A GRANDPA!"

"This is the happiest day of my life!"

Squeals of laughter and the sound of joyful tears suddenly filled the house.

Alec and I were quickly surrounded and embraced...and squeezed...and kissed...rinse, repeat.

~*~*~*~

Alec and I, with our parents in tow, went back to the doctor at fourteen weeks, hoping that our little peanut's face would be visible enough to show any signs of TCS. But the ultrasound was still unclear.

That led to our appointment three weeks later.

At seventeen weeks pregnant, I was lying on the exam table clutching Alec's hand for dear life. We had talked about this moment on many occasions, but the reality was much harder than either of us could have expected.

We had informed our parents that we needed to go to this

particular ultrasound alone…just the two of us. We needed to be able to process things as a couple, no matter what the outcome, then we would let everyone else know.

Respectfully, they all said they understood.

Alec and I both had our eyes glued to the screen as the ultrasound technician was sliding the transducer wand over my expanding belly. We got to hear the baby's heartbeat, which caused me to burst into tears. Damn pregnancy hormones.

"The heartbeat is steady and strong," the technician said sweetly. "But…hmm." She paused and stopped moving the wand as she leaned closer to the screen. "Can you shift onto your side for me, Mrs. Cavanaugh? Just for a moment."

"Oh no!" I blurted out. "Is something wrong? Is our baby okay?"

The technician turned back around, her face never giving anything away. "I just need to get a different angle. Everything is fine."

Alec and I nodded at each other as I rolled over to my right side, making sure that I was facing the screen.

"Alright, let me just take a look here…" The technician rolled the wand over my skin, pressing a bit harder than she was before. Then she clicked a button on the keyboard and let out a small laugh. "Well, you little stinker!" she whispered.

"What? What is it?" I asked anxiously.

"I'm not sure how the other techs missed this, but…it appears that you're having twins."

"WHAT?!" Alec and I both said in unison.

"Twins?" I repeated. "Are you…are you sure?"

The technician slid her chair back so we could see more of the screen. "This little bubble here, that's Baby A…and then over here, hiding behind their sibling, we have Baby B." She paused. "I know you're here to find out about the Treacher Collins gene, but first, would you like to know the genders?"

Alec and I both glanced at each other as our smiles widened.

"Yes, we would!" Alec replied. He squeezed my hand tighter.

"Alright," the technician stated cheerfully. She jiggled my belly a few times to get our precious bundles of joy to shift a bit so that they weren't right on top of each other. "Okay, so you can see that the legs are crossed on Baby A...and here are the knees, then the little feet. All ten toes are accounted for." She clicked a button to pause the screen and smiled. "Baby A...is a boy!"

"A boy..." I whispered unbelievably.

Alec and I locked tear-filled eyes. He instantly leaned over and kissed my forehead. "We're having a son!" he whispered. Then he kissed me again. "Our little miracle."

"Alright," the technician rubbed her hands together. "Let's see if we can get Baby B to cooperate as well."

Fifteen minutes later, Baby B was still being stubborn, keeping their legs crossed and hiding behind Baby A. But just as we were about to call it quits, the twins switched positions.

"Oh...oh...wait!" the technician blurted out excitedly. "Legs are uncrossing...aaaaaaand...just a bit more, little one...oh...we have...a girl! Congratulations! One of each!"

I couldn't speak. I was crying too hard.

"A son...and a daughter!" Alec cried out. "I can't believe this!"

At that moment, nothing else mattered. Whatever the outcome, our hearts were full.

"Two little miracles," I squeaked.

Alec leaned over and kissed my forehead again. "I love you so much...so damn much!"

A laugh escaped through my tears. "I love you, more!"

The technician smiled. "I just need to check a few more measurements," she announced. "Then we'll have a better idea if either baby has TCS."

We watched in awe as she measured each of their little heads. Then she went on to the bones in their tiny arms, followed by their long legs…all perfectly proportioned.

A few minutes later, she wiped off the gel and turned toward us with an unreadable expression. "Well, Mr. and Mrs. Cavanaugh, both Baby A's and Baby B's growth rates look right on target…"

"Do they have the syndrome?" Alec asked eagerly.

The technician reached out to touch our clutched hands. "Baby B is perfectly healthy. I didn't see any signs of Treacher Collins on any of her scans." Then the technician's expression changed. "Baby A, however, I'm almost ninety-five percent certain that he has the syndrome. I'm sorry."

Round two for the waterworks.

Alec and I left the doctor's office with ultrasound pictures in our hands. We sat in our car in the parking lot and stared at the grainy black and white images.

Then we cried.

There were tears of happiness that we had been blessed with not just one, but two little miracles. And then there were tears of sadness, knowing that our son may have to endure things that no parent would ever wish upon their child.

But even so…we were so in love with both of our sweet babies, and couldn't wait for their arrival.

When we got home, we took turns calling our parents to tell them the news. As expected, it was mixed emotions for them as well. But happiness definitely outweighed anything else.

CHAPTER 31

Nearing the end of my second trimester, it was getting harder and harder for me to work. Being six months pregnant with twins was definitely taking its toll on my body, not to mention the fact that Alec and I had recently bought a new house...one big enough to raise a family, with a huge backyard, and lots of space for Sarge to run...so there was a lot of packing and unpacking and setting things up.

I was worn out.

I loved my job and my co-workers so much, but I guess I pushed myself further than I probably should have.

One afternoon, I had a stabbing pain in my lower back that just would not let up. So, after a few hours of enduring it, I told my boss that I needed to go home. He made sure I got to my car safely, and then told me that he thought it was time for me to take a leave of absence and get some rest.

I was in so much discomfort that I agreed without another thought. I stopped at the grocery store on my way home and picked up several packages of strawberries and Muenster cheese. Yay pregnancy cravings!

As I pulled into our driveway, I noticed Alec's car was parked in its usual spot. *How odd*, I thought to myself. *I figured he had work today.* When I came around the bend, three more cars came into view. My parents', Alec's parents', and Liza's. *Okay, something is definitely up.*

I parked and waddled up the steps, carrying my delicious goodies. When I opened the front door, I heard noises and laughter coming from upstairs. So, after putting away my strawberries and cheese, I slowly made my way up, having to pause to take a breath after every two to three steps. It was in those moments that I wished we had an elevator.

I made it to the top landing and had to take a few minutes to slow my breathing.

The voices seemed to be coming from the end of the hall…which was going to be our double nursery until the twins were old enough to sleep separately.

"Alec?" I called out as I finally made it to the doorway.

My gorgeous husband spun around, nearly tripping over a paint can in his rush to get to me. "Sweetheart, are you okay?" He reached for my stomach as if to cradle and protect his unborn children. "Are the babies alright? What are you doing home so early?"

"I'm fine. We're fine. I just…I had some lower back pain again, so I came home."

He sighed with his hands on his hips. "You're doing too much! Why didn't you call me? I would have picked you up!"

I smiled at my overly-protective husband. "I am perfectly capable of driving myself home. I even stopped at the store first."

He lovingly glared at me. "Strawberries and cheese again?"

I grinned and nodded.

He sighed. "I think it's time for you to take your pregnancy leave. And I want you to call the doctor about the pain. We're not taking any chances here."

I ran my fingers gently through his hair. "Okay. I will, first thing in the morning."

Alec sighed again and gently caressed my face. "Thank you." Then his perfect smile crept across his lips as he gestured all around him. "Well...since you came home early and ruined your surprise, what do you think?"

I glanced around the room. He, Liza, and both of our parents, were covered in dark grey and mint-green paint. The beige carpet had finally been put down, and both of the dark-cherry cribs were put together, set up on either side of our custom-made changing table. Pastel yellow stars of all sizes were painted above each crib, with the words *Sometimes Miracles Come In Pairs* written in between.

My emotions instantly overflowed, as they did quite often those days. I cried out of happiness and excitement, then gave each of my amazing family members a hug. "This looks incredible," I whimpered. "I love it."

Alec wrapped his arm around my shoulder and gave me a little squeeze. "I'm so glad you do."

~*~*~*~

Two months later, just shy of being three weeks early, at 4:33pm, Aurora Grace made her debut into this crazy world, followed by her brother, Klarc Alexander, precisely ten minutes later at 4:43pm. Both of them had a head full of black hair and the brightest blue eyes you could imagine, just like their gorgeous daddy.

It turned out that Klarc did, in fact, have TCS, but according to the doctors, it was a very mild case. His ears were nearly fully formed, and his hearing ended up being 80% in one ear, and 90% in the other, so the likelihood that he would need a hearing aid was very low. He was taken to the NICU as a precaution, but was given a clean bill of health within a few hours.

As I sat there in my hospital bed, with a sleeping baby in each arm, I glanced up at Alec. He was staring back at me with a dreamy look in his eyes that was so serene...so content...so proud.

He lowered himself onto the bed, careful not to wake

either of our sweet babies. Then he took a moment to caress each of their faces before focusing his gaze on me. "I never thought that I could ever love you more than I already do…but right now, I feel like I've fallen in love with you all over again." He paused as he leaned over to gently kiss my forehead. "This is the happiest I have ever been in my life, and I can't wait for whatever the future holds for us."

My eyes glistened. "I love you, too, Alec. Forever and always."

Alec grinned. "As you wish."

THE END.

ABOUT THE AUTHOR

If you are interested to learn more about Dani Healy,
visit her website: www.danihealyfiction.com

ABOUT THE
CHARACTER ARTIST

If you are interested to learn more about Jennie Lyne Hiott,
look for her on facebook: JennieLyneFiction

Want more from Dani Healy'? Check out The Cursed One:

Unknowingly, she fell in love with the one thing that terrified her the most...

When Avery Miller met Sebastian Taylor on that cold October night, she was sure that fate had somehow brought them together; but now that his secrets are finally unraveling, she is coming to terms with the fact that their destiny may be darker than she ever imagined.

The truth is, Sebastian has been hiding from the Pure Ones (immortal gods who have had their purity stolen) for nearly a century, fearful of what they might do if they were to discover his location. But now a series of unforeseen circumstances have forced him to choose between the life he wants and the life he was 'cursed' to endure forever.

Ages 15+ for violent/torturous imagery.
Available at Amazon.com in both paperback and kindle.

ACKNOWLEDGEMENTS

I have to give a HUGE shout out to my amazingly talented editing/support team (aka my friends and family all over the world)!

My mama
My Godmom
My "huggy-buggy"
Wa'el Jom'aa
Mohammed Al Mohammed Al Sibahi
John Gerlach
Kate Ford
Jennie Lyne Hiott
Lynn Floyd
Ahmed Saber Elshazly

You all gave me insights into things that I never would have thought about…adding bits and pieces, or sometimes even large chunks lol…to certain scenes that ended up completely changing the story and making it into the beautiful tale of love and faith that it is today! You all pushed me to better myself with each passing chapter, never allowing me to settle for anything less than my best. So, from the bottom of my heart, thank you! I love you all so much! *squeeze hugs*

And thank YOU, the reader, for taking the time to give my story a chance! I hope you enjoyed going on this journey with me, Alec, and Scarlett! *hugs*

AlecPhantom